The Other Shakespeare

Lea Rachel

Published by Writer's Design

For all the strong women in my life

but most especially for my mother

Sara Bahar

1

Every third birth shall be for the grave. The words rang in Judith Shakespeare's ears as she picked up the looking glass with the ornate, gold trimmed handle, and spied again her heavy blond locks and clear blue eyes. It was always startling, to see her own face reflected in such sharp outline and detail. It was nothing like looking in the waters of the Avon, the cold dark waters which rushed by with such urgent speed, ferrying leaves and branches and thick clumps of dirt on their way to the next village, her visage in the current too broken and cracked to grasp. Judith liked looking in the glass, as if into the eyes of a stranger, a petite, pretty, but somewhat distant stranger whose mysteries had yet to be discovered. Though every time she did she couldn't help but also remember the words her mother had cried to her father before she begged him to give the gift away: *Every third birth shall be for the grave.*

"'Tis nonsense," her father had said, trying to tease his wife, Mary, into not worrying so much about the silly predictions of a soothsayer more than sixteen years before.

"She stopped the deaths," Mary reminded him, almost afraid to acknowledge this truth out loud.

1

John nodded, grateful as well that the potion the white witch had given them had stopped the deaths of their children. After John, their first, had died even before making it past the lying-in, and Margaret, their second, had died before a full sun had passed, he had been nearly as upset as his wife over the inability of their children to hold onto life. But now they had five beautiful issues: Judith, William, Gilbert, Joan and Anne, all alive, all healthy, all proving the witch's prophecy that for every three births one child would have to die, wrong. He wished Mary would just let it go already. She held on to this prospect of future grief like the truly devout held onto a well worn set of rosary beads, clicking and counting them all day long. More than anything, John was annoyed that his expensive gift of a beautifully wrought Italian hand mirror, which he'd paid nearly ten pounds for on his previous trip to Coventry, was being spurned by his wife.

"I can't keep it," she pleaded, "it reminds me too much of the witch's mirror. I beseech you, take it back."

Instead, John had given the gift to his oldest daughter, Judith, for use as a prop in her games of playacting. And every time she went out to the forest with the rest of her brothers and sisters to put on a show, she couldn't help but look into it.

"Judith," William Shakespeare called, walking up to his older sister, "have you chosen the props for today's play yet?"

Judith quickly folded the looking glass into its linen cover. She could hear her younger brothers and sisters laughing and shouting in the clearing behind her. It was another warm summer afternoon, the trees thick with foliage, the scent of mint and sweetbriar strong in the air, the give of pliant dirt soft beneath her knees. She picked out a few props from the pile before her and walked with William back to the space where her other brother, Gilbert, and her two sisters, Joan and Anne, were waiting.

She handed Gilbert the gnarled oak cane, indicating that he got to play the gouty king for a second week in a row. Gilbert grinned in appreciation and thrust the cane hard into the ground before him. Judith bestowed the queen's crown made of braided twigs and bindweed on her sister Joan, who smiled broadly and worked to pin the crown into her long brown hair. Anne, the youngest and littlest of the Shakespeare children, Judith gave the fan made of chicken feather and string.

"Hold this up when I tell you to," she instructed. "You shall be the cover that the maid and the prince hide behind when they seek to run away."

Anne nodded seriously, glad to have been given a role in the production and determined to do a good job.

"And you William," Judith said, walking over to the brother closest in age to herself, "you shall be the prince." She handed him the wooden sword they'd whittled out of a piece of elm. It had a long leather strap wrapped around the handle which William carefully unraveled and rewound around his stomach, so that the sword hung from his side in the manner of a true gentleman.

"Wait! Wait! Anon, don't forget me!" Running up the path, nearly tripping over a tree root, was Richard Whateley, their neighbor. He always wanted to be a part of the Shakespeare family games, even when he wasn't actually invited. Judith sighed, but then walked over to the pile of props and chose for Richard a threadbare black hat. He would be the prince's man-in-waiting, his lookout, when the prince and the maid made their escape.

Judith carefully laid the rest of the items aside, the old teething coral that was handy as a magic wand, the dirty white gloves rescued from their father's workshop, the clubs, shields, and knives made of wood, leather, and stuffed cloth that the children had put a lot of time and effort into crafting. She arranged Gilbert and Joan in the middle of the clearing, facing each other but turned slightly askance, and then gave the signal to start the performance.

"My true and honorable wife," Gilbert began, his head held high like the king he thought he was. "My faithful helpmate, why do you forsake me now? Why do you choose a son's love over a husband's? Over your kingdom's? The people will not stand for an errant prince and an ignoble princess. She must be sent away and he must be made to do his duty; to his family and to the throne." Gilbert paused and leant on his cane, "I insist on being the master of what is mine own. My goods, my chattel, my fields, and most certainly," he eyed his wife, "my son."

"Yes, thy husband," Joan replied, her eyes downcast but her voice strong. Judith was pleased with the effort; Joan had finally struck the right balance between the demure, respectful wife, and the strong-willed, determined queen.

Judith sat on a tree stump and watched - her part as the maid wouldn't come on for a few more acts anyway. William entered the scene and engaged the king and queen in an argument. "Never doubt that I love her," he told his parents, chin held high. "Doubt that the stars are fire, doubt that the sun does move, doubt truth to be a liar, but never doubt my love." Judith was reminded, again, of William's ability to develop a phrase. All she had to do was feed him an idea and he came up with poetry inspired phrases. She sat back and crossed her arms and watched the rest of the scene play out.

Judith had been directing her younger brothers and sisters in "playacting" (as their father liked to call it), in "nuisance" (is how their mother referred to it), for as long as she could remember. From the time she could walk she was picking things up around the house and playing with them in rich stories of make-believe secretly imagined. When her brother William was born she immediately took to dressing him and feeding him and talking to him about all the things that went on in her head. As soon as he could walk Judith used him as a prop in her games, and after he began to talk, Judith gave him well-defined roles. William liked playing the part of a soldier, or even a fool, but oddly, he never liked being king. When Gilbert, Joan, and Anne were born one right after the other a few years later, Judith finally had the beginnings of a troupe where she could put on full productions.

Which the children did, nearly every Sunday afternoon after church. After the priest had finished his sermon and the Symons twins in the row ahead of them had been woken up with a loud rap on the knuckles, Gilbert poked William and William poked Joan and all the Shakespeare children rushed to be the first out of the cold stone building. They sprinted home, the hot afternoon sun warming their cold limbs and backsides sore from the hard, damp pews. In the summertime the luscious greens of Stratford's streets displaced the images of the whitewashed church walls from their memory, the eerie walls which tried, but didn't quite cover, the illicit Catholic paintings from before King Henry's time. Once at home, out of their Sunday best and triumphant again in their rumpled day clothes, the children would finish their chores and then head out together as a group to the forest. Judith, William, Gilbert, and Joan carried the props from the shed behind the house, while Anne dragged the wool blanket she needed when she got sleepy. The children walked to a clearing where they knew they could talk and shout as loudly as they wanted, and no adults would beat them for it.

"But I fail to understand," Richard said to Judith after the story they'd been acting came to an end. "Why did the prince and the maid have to seek shelter in France? Couldn't they have stayed at court and married? Didn't the king and queen understand that they were in love?"

"They understood. It mattered not."

Richard looked crestfallen.

"Sometimes love is not enough," Judith said, more patiently this time. "In this instance, the kingdom was more important. Preserving the family line and not marrying an inappropriate commoner was - and is - more important than anything else."

"'Tis sad," Richard couldn't help but say, even though he knew it made him look babyish.

"Be glad you're not royalty, nor even a wealthy nobleman," Judith remonstrated. "They have to marry whom their parents tell them to. At least when you're without braveries, you can fall in love with anyone."

Richard squinted into the sun. He had never thought of that. His parents were always complaining that they didn't have enough money for pottage, or pie, or a decent cup of ale; that if only they had more money they could buy some linen and set a respectable table. Richard couldn't count how many times he'd watched his parents yell at each other over who had spent the last farthing, it was so often. It was a revelation to him to think that being poor could actually be better in some ways. Judith always said the oddest things. He'd have to think this one over for awhile, before he could be sure Judith wasn't just leading him by the nose.

"'Tis time to go," William said, approaching the two of them. "We don't want to get mother angry again for being late."

By the time they arrived back home Mary was indeed waiting for them, watching from behind the latticed windows that let in a bit of a draft at the front of the house. When she saw her children approach at last she counted the heads of each of them to make sure they were all there, and then she struggled with how to welcome her children back home. On the one hand, she wanted to run out and greet them and embrace them all for returning to her alive and healthy. On the other hand, she wanted to yell at them for being gone so long, for taking little Anne with them yet again when obviously she was too young to be out in the sun all afternoon, and for not seeming to care how much their absence worried their mother. Mary loved her children, but she'd had no idea before becoming a mother how much they would worry her too.

The door opened with a creak like split wood and William spoke first. "Mother, you should see our new play. Gilbert plays an old king brilliantly and Joan is superb as a stupid, irresponsible queen." William and Joan glanced at each other and broke out in grins. "I have a hard time remembering all the things I'm supposed to say, but I get to brandish a sword in the second act and I've been perfecting my swordfight for weeks." William struck a combative pose. "See now, when I step forward with my right foot, I can stab good with my right hand. But I'm left handed so it doesn't feel right. Now, if I step forward with my left foot, and stab with my left hand, it goes much better. See?" Mary watched her son prance around the room aggressively stabbing the air. When he finally stopped she looked into the face of her bursting child and wondered where he got all his energy. Was she ever this happy, she wondered, when she was a child?

"Go inside and study your Latin," she commended. With a sigh, William turned and went upstairs.

Judith stepped inside and tried to head up the stairs after her brother, but her mother stopped her. "We need more wood," she told her, "and when you're done fetching that you can help with the laundry."

Without a word Judith handed the props in her hands to her sister, brushed the dirt off her skirts, and headed out towards the back of the house to the wood pile. She brought in two heavy armloads and set them carefully by the hearth. Then she went behind the garden, where the large black laundry pot steamed with hot water. Judith picked up the wooden paddle her mother had abandoned a few minutes earlier and stirred the clothes in the hot, lye-filled water. Immediately, she felt the ache of it in her shoulders and back.

It had been a beautiful day. The orange-tinged summer sun had been hot all afternoon, but the heat had been tempered with a cool breeze and a scatter of clouds that broke up the bright sky. Judith looked out over the horizon, at the green rolling hills of Warwick and the graying thatched rooftops of her neighbors and watched as two vultures circled the air in a kind of dance, dipping low and then climbing high, and then dipping low all over again. She knew they were searching for kill, seeking out food and sniffing for blood, but from a distance it looked like a game, like they were engaged in a graceful, perpetual courtship with the winds.

Shifting from her right to her left foot, a flicker of resentment passed through Judith at again being given the hardest work in the house. But then it passed. Judith stared into the hot, dark water of the pot and began making up a new story in her head. It opened with a scene of witches, faces long and noses hooked, hair all about in a tangled jumble, stirring a pot of potion and casting fortunes. *Double, double, toil and trouble...fire burn and cauldron bubble...scale of dragon, tooth of woolf...witches' mummy, maw and gulf.* Judith giggled to herself, wondering what indeed witches put into their potions.

Mary came out then and sat on a stool, watching her daughter work. Her feet ached and her hands were tired from kneading dough earlier in the afternoon and she couldn't help but wonder with annoyance why Judith looked so lost, as if in another world. If she wasn't playing games, her eldest daughter couldn't seem to concentrate on anything. Mary sighed audibly while taking in Judith's dirty skirts and tousled appearance and thought, if only she took care of herself better she could be so pretty. With that lovely ivory skin and fine yellow hair, if only she would protect them from the sun like I ask her to. Mary again regretted that she'd allowed Judith to spend the entire afternoon traipsing about in the forest, getting her kirtle dirty and play-acting with a bunch of children. She sized up her daughter's well-proportioned figure and confirmed again that she shouldn't be doing that, not at her age. Judith was past sixteen years and almost a woman now.

Mary cleared her throat. "Is your sampler finished yet?"

Judith looked up and focused her thoughts on the needlework. Most nights after supper, as the family gathered around the hearth, Judith was increasingly expected to say nothing and concentrate on her needlework. Right now she was completing a border, a pattern of birds and flowers that her mother had earlier passed on to her, but she didn't like how it was turning out. The beak on the hummingbird was far too long, and the flowers had somehow bunched together, as if they were huddling together for support from some collective fear. It always distressed Judith a little to have to pick up the sampler at night and assess again her embroidery skills, because in all honesty, whether her mother chose to admit it or not, she simply wasn't very good at stitching.

"I'll work on it after supper," Judith suggested.

"You need to spend more time on it than you do. It takes years to put together a good trousseau, and right now yours has very few things in it." Mary said this believing that both she, and her daughter, regularly thought about Judith's eventual wedding day.

Judith paused again from her work. When she thought about getting married she imagined a warm day, lots of flowers in bloom and birds in the air, a fun march through town with the musicians and children throwing coins after her. A few years ago Judith had made up a story that included a wedding procession - the only problem had been when they tried to act it out Joan and Gilbert kept getting distracted, laughing and tripping over each other and not taking the thing seriously at all. They had simply been too young. Judith had given up on that play, but now she thought about bringing it back. Joan and Gilbert were older now and it would be fun to stage another mock wedding.

"What color shall your wedding gown be?" Mary asked, following her own internal train of thought.

"What color do you prefer?" Judith inquired, trying to give the choice to her mother like a gift.

"By my life child, 'tis your wedding. You should have a preference."

Judith tried to recall what color her mother had told her her own wedding gown had been. She thought that if she picked the same color as her mother had, it would make her happy. But she simply could not remember what her mother had chosen. "Yellow?"

Yellow? Didn't the girl realize that a light color would wash out her face and hair? Red would contrast much better. If I suggested she wear a veil, Mary thought, I imagine she'd go along with that, even though no one wears veils anymore.

By her mother's silence Judith knew she had chosen wrong. She wanted to please her mother, she just seemed to keep messing up with her more and more instead. "How about a veil? Shall I wear a veil on my wedding day?"

Mary let out a tick of exasperation. How could she make her daughter understand the importance of her own wedding? Everyone knew that the path to true happiness was a good, sound marriage, but her daughter didn't seem to care about such things at all. All her daughter cared about were stories, plays, and childish games - nothing that would lead to a good man or a good marriage. Mary sighed and looked upwards. By heaven, what did God have in store for this daughter of hers, and when would He make it plain?

Mary eventually stood up to go into the house. Before turning around she glanced again at her eldest daughter. "You must needs keep your cap on when you go out into the forest, Judith. Otherwise your hair gets loose and unruly."

Judith nodded solemnly. "Yes, mother."

By the time Judith had finished rinsing, squeezing, and hanging the laundry to dry, supper was ready. She entered the house rubbing her chapped, raw hands and joined her family at the table. William and Gilbert had already begun a game of Word Make-Up when Judith sat down on the bench across from them. Mary was busy dishing out portions of steaming meat pie to their father at the other end of the table.

"Marigoistic," William whispered, giving Gilbert a challenging look.

Gilbert rolled his eyes and Joan, sitting beside Judith, couldn't help but let out a soft groan. It was an easy one, just the flower marigold turned into a description. William had a soft spot for flowers, trees and birds. He loved the outdoors and was always making up words based on the beautiful things he found there. The only problem was that, by now, everyone knew it. And of course, with a smug expression on his face, Gilbert immediately offered as a definition, "A person who is marigoistic is warm, golden, and in full bloom, like a flower."

"Ach, too easy," Joan ruled, her mouth full of food. She never felt much compunction about stating her opinions, handing them out at the supper table like passing driftwood. "You should be more creative when William favors you with an easy one." Gilbert pouted and everyone quieted down as their father glanced in their direction.

John Shakespeare had dark brown eyes and light brown hair, the color of which blended seamlessly into his earth brown jerkin and dirty white smock. His hands were rough and permanently streaked with tannin but his smooth face, generally graced with a smile, belied the hard life his callused hands implied. Judith looked at her father as she chewed her food and wondered what he thought about all day as he boiled pigskin and hammered leather into flat, malleable shapes. She wanted to ask him what his days were like, so she could use the information in a future story, but she knew better than to speak up at the supper table.

"Irappy," Gilbert whispered a few minutes later, now that it was his turn to make up a word. It never took Gilbert long to come up with a word because in the summertime, when the weather was hot and it was difficult to sleep at night, he passed the time lying in bed making up as many words as he could. William, Gilbert noted competitively, always took longer to come up with his words.

William recognized the Latin in the prefix to the word and immediately thought of the obvious definition - irate and happy put together, a feeling of mixed anger and joy. He hesitated in giving out this answer though, because while it was at least as good as Gilbert's last one, he knew he could do better. Besides, Joan was being particularly judgmental over the obvious answers that evening, so William felt he had to take his time and think harder. His brow creased and he played with his food while he tried to come up with something smart, yet witty, something that would make his sister proud.

"Finish your stew," Mary admonished, noticing how little William had eaten. Cocking her head to the side she asked, "Are you two playing that word game again?"

William and Gilbert looked down into their laps while Judith stole a quick glance at their father. He was draining his mug of ale, seemingly oblivious to the drama unfolding around him. Mary reminded her children how God had worked to provide them with food. How their Creator was munificent and kind and should not be taken for granted. John eventually put his bread down on the table, turned to his sons and asked, "What 'tis the word?"

At first, no one replied, so John asked the question again.

"Irappy," Gilbert admitted. "I gave it to William."

William met his father's eyes and at that moment it came to him. "The look in a thirsty dog's eye when you give him a fresh bowl of milk - that's irappy."

Joan let out a squeal of delight before clapping her hands over her mouth. Judith nodded in approval. Their father guffawed with pleasure and William blushed a light pink, knowing he had done well. Mary, annoyed at the lack of discipline around her table but not wanting to contradict her husband's enjoyment of it, got up and went to bring over a bowl of fruit from the sideboard. A subdued Gilbert sat still in his chair. He hated being bested. He took a breath and was about to say something, to argue a point, when Anne let out a loud, rasping cough. The family watched as her whole body shook with the effort.

"'Tis- 'tis fine," she struggled ineffectively to say. Anne had always been a fragile girl, taking extra naps during the day and never being able to play in the forest quite as long as her older siblings, but she had never been worrisomely sick, and she had certainly never had a coughing fit like this one before. It gathered strength until, with a pop, a thick globule of blood flew out of her mouth and landed with a splash in the middle of the table. For a minute, everyone just stared at it.

Mary was the first to react, jumping to her daughter's side and grabbing her head in her hands, searching Anne's eyes for the illness within. Judith rushed to find a handkerchief while Joan held on to her sister's hand and pressed its cool palm between her own. Anne had a confused expression on her face, surprised as anyone about what had just happened. She knew she had been feeling extra tired lately, and chilled even in the middle of a hot afternoon, but it had never seemed all that important.

Mary grunted as she lifted Anne up in her arms and carried her to the box chair by the hearth. It was the chair that Mary had comforted all the Shakespeare children in when they were first born, and through all their childhood illnesses. Its brown seat was worn smooth and round and its arms were covered in nicks and scratches where all the children had, at some point, dug their nails and teeth into it.

Mary held her daughter to her chest, patted her back, and cooed into her ear. After a few minutes Anne's frail body relaxed. She looked about her and smiled, sinking into her mother's embrace. Joan took a seat on the floor at her mother's feet and the rest of the family gathered together around them. Anne seemed fine and there was no longer any evidence of blood or coughing, but the mood in the room was no longer joyful; the word game had ended and no one seemed to know what to do with themselves. Judith wished she could tell a story, something to distract everybody's mind and maybe make them all smile, but she knew her mother would not approve. Their father stood off to the side, picking dirt from beneath his fingernails with the tip of a knife.

A heavy knock at the front door broke the silence and made everyone but Anne jump as if they'd been hit with a poker. Mary looked inquisitively at her husband who lifted his shoulders as if he had no idea who it might be. In truth, his gut told him that it was Langrake, come to collect the money from the illegal wool trade the week before. Unbeknownst to his family John had begun brogging, and in the last few months the business had grown out of his control. He hadn't meant to enter the underground wool trading business, it had all started as a one-time favor to Mary's rich uncle Edward who asked him, innocently enough, to drop off a tod on one of his trips to Coventry. But when John handed off the wool and collected the heavy sack of gold in return, the weight of it told him that something was wrong. He let it bounce a few times in his hand and calculated that the pouch must contain over two hundred pounds of coin, but before he could stop the toothless merchant to let him know that a mistake had been made, the man was gone and the realization of what had happened settled on John's shoulders. When Edward asked him a month later to make the trade again, John, to his own surprise, consented. Thinking back on it, John had justified the transaction as merely his due. He considered the span of his life and proudly saw his rise from lowly country farmer to successful town glover. He had married well, into a family that could trace its lineage back to the Domesday Book of William the Conqueror, and had then made his way through a succession of important municipal positions from ale-taster to constable to chamberlain to bailiff, and now even alderman. Taken together, it all seemed a natural progression. And now John was being given the opportunity to make the kind of money that fit his ambitions. He couldn't deny that he enjoyed spending the coin the wool trades brought in. He could afford all manner of things now that, without asking where they came from, even Mary enjoyed. But when the heavy knock rang out again at the front door, John could not help but fear that the day of reckoning had arrived. His wife was always saying that God kept a tally, and he was sure that the paymaster had come at last.

"Shall I get it?" William asked. John shook his head and lifted himself heavily from the wall. He went to the front door and pulled it open to find a flurry of scarlet red cloaks and crimson velvet liveries. He jumped when a trumpet rang out loud and clear off to his right. John smiled then, his fears dissolving into self-righteous appraisal. He was the chief alderman of Stratford-upon-Avon and another group of traveling players had come to his door seeking permission to perform. It was one of John's favorite responsibilities as alderman of Stratford, to approve any acting troupe that came to town and asked for permission to put on a performance. It was merely a formality, of course, as he would never turn down a request from a powerful patron, and this time it appeared to be the Earl of Worcester's Men who had made their way to town, but John dutifully inspected the players' letters and listened to the list of titles the troupe was ready to put on. John considered pretending to turn the players down, just to tease his children whom he knew were listening in the hall behind him, but he was too relieved that the knock at the door wasn't Langrake that he had nothing but gratitude for anyone who faced him. He offered generous terms to the players' manager, shook his hand, and then agreed to a first performance in the guildhall on the morrow.

As John closed the door and faced his family, he could still hear the bells on the players' girtles clinking and chiming as they made their way down the street. Judith and William were standing upright against the back wall, Judith's hands clasped together, William seeming not to breathe. Gilbert and Joan were smiling too, but it was the look of irappiness radiating from Anne's face that gave John the most pleasure. "Alas," he asked, "who would like to see a play tomorrow?"

2

The next day dawned bright and yellow, as warm and cloudless as the day before. Judith set the hoe against a tree and pushed her hair from her eyes. She'd been gardening all morning, waiting for the time to pass until she could pick her brothers up from school. She surveyed the ground around her and judged that while she had gotten a lot done, her mother would still not be satisfied. The herb garden had yet to be weeded and the side fencing still needed to be repaired where the rabbits had burrowed a path underneath. But there was always tomorrow and Judith would be sure to wake early and start again first thing in the morning. The opening performance of the Worcester's Men was scheduled for later that afternoon and shops were closing early, work was being put on hold, and children were being let out of school well before the supper hour. Judith wanted to finish gardening early enough so that she could go to the schoolhouse and be there to walk her brothers home.

It wasn't as though her brothers *needed* to be walked home anymore, although sometimes Judith liked to pretend they were still so young that they did. It was more that if Judith caught her brothers just as the lessons ended she could often get them to tell her about what they'd learned. And she loved hearing about the things they'd learned. Judith had been meeting her brothers at the side yard next to the school house since their mother was too heavy with Joan to do it herself, and by now it had become a regular thing. They took the long way home, by the river Avon, and William and Gilbert alternately recited for her the lessons they'd gone over in school that day - the grammar exercises, the Latin readings, the recitations.

As Judith made her way towards the house to wash her hands and put away her dirty apron, she recalled the moral proverbs her brothers had shared with her last week. She had a hard time remembering the Latin, but the English translations always stuck. "Say Little at Banquets," was a favorite, but "Judge Fairly," and "Overcome thy Parent with Patience," rang remarkably true. Judith sometimes wondered what Cato, the author of the proverbs, must have been like. Was he tall or small, bearded or plain, did he love his mother or have as much difficulty pleasing her as she herself did?

Judith stepped inside the house and made her way up the stairs to the bed chamber she shared with her sisters, thinking about Cato as a character she could put into a play. She poured a basin of water into the dry sink and toweled her hands and face.

"Tarry not on the way home," Mary called from down the hall.

"Yes, mother."

Judith neatly folded the towel in half and hung it back on the rail by the side of the basin. She opened a window and threw the dirty water outside. Then she tied a fresh cap on her head, slipped downstairs and out of the house, and walked briskly down Henley Street.

The sun beat heavily upon her brow and there wasn't much of a relenting breeze, but Judith felt happy to be away from the house and on her way to school. She only wished she'd taken a draught of water before she'd left.

Turning onto Church Street Judith heard, before she saw, the cluster of mothers standing outside the guildhall, chatting amongst themselves. The grounds were otherwise quiet which meant that the boys were still inside taking their lessons. Judith wanted to keep to herself so she stayed away from the building and sought out the shade of a tree across the street. From where she sat she could still see the external stairs that reached to the top-floor schoolroom, so she'd know the minute the boys were let out. Judith relaxed and closed her eyes and recalled asking her father once, a very long time ago, if she could go to school too.

"But girls don't go to school," her father had said, chuckling to himself.

"Why not?"

"Dear child, what good would it do a girl to learn Latin and Greek or the arts of rhetoric?"

Judith said nothing, wondering what good it would do William and Gilbert to learn all of those things.

"D'you fancy going into politics when you get older?" her father continued, his grin widening, "perhaps the church?"

"Perhaps."

Her father's mirth suddenly turned serious. "Judith, daughter, everyone has a place in this world. God has made it so. And yours, as a young lady, is not in school. You must learn many things in this life, but you will learn them by following your mother's example. Cooking, gardening, cleaning, needlework - these are not idle occupations. Nor are they easily done well. Your time is better spent learning how to keep a house, then reading Seneca or Aristotle or some of those other foolish amusements." Her father ended his lecture with a heartfelt smile, but it didn't make Judith feel any better. She was still confused, and now, hurt. Did God really divine that boys deserved to go to school while girls didn't? And if he did, why? Judith's face stung with the knowledge, somewhere deep inside her, that she was being told she wasn't as good as a boy child.

John bent down and drew his daughter into an awkward embrace. "Sweet Judith," he said, holding her out in front of him again, "in truth, school 'tisn't much fun. You have to memorize page after page of old, sometimes silly poetry, and if you're called on to recite and make even a single mistake, the master beats you. D'you remember those welts on Gilbert's arm last week?"

Judith winced at the memory of the string of red bumps along her brother's inner forearm.

"Most boys prefer to stay at home than go to school, and you want to go to school rather than stay at home!"

Judith smiled to please her father. "Can- can you tutor me? At least how to read and write the letters? I would very much like to be able to study the bible," Judith added, thinking the proposal sounded better if she sounded devoted.

"Nay, Judith, 'tisn't possible. I'm busy all day in the workshop, or at the guildhouse, if not traveling to Gloucester or Warwick."

But Judith was suddenly stuck on the idea of learning at home. "Mother can read a little, can she not?"

"She can," John admitted. "She mastered a bit when she was a child." He looked into his daughter's eyes and continued with grave seriousness, "But do not ask your mother to teach you."

Judith understood that it would be a mistake to bother her mother with this. All her mother wanted her to do was cook or clean or sew. Judith wiped her eyes and tried to look happy for her father.

"Besides," John added, "'tis costly to go to school. You need ink and paper and candles. Those goods n'aren't cheap."

Judith had never thought about the cost of going to school. It hadn't even occurred to her.

"Always remember that your mother and I do our best to provide all that you need," John said, standing up. "You wouldn't be happy going to school, 'tis a surety. Imagine being the only girl in the room, surrounded by all those dirty, obnoxious little boys. And then, say perchance you did learn to read and write and study the great poets, what would you do with that knowledge? Nay, it wouldn't help you get a husband. In fact, many men might be turned away by a woman brandishing airs. If you went down that path, my daughter, you would not be happy."

Judith hadn't thought about the practical aspects of going to school. Of sitting in a room with only boys, of trying to recite her lessons and everyone looking at her. Just the thought of it shamed her and brought color to her cheeks. Maybe her father was right, maybe it wouldn't bring her happiness, although Judith had never thought about such a question before. All she knew was that deep down, she wanted to go to school; she wanted to read. She couldn't explain why, she couldn't argue the merits of it, she just knew that it was a desire deep within her, without explanation, without reason. Considerations of happiness simply didn't enter into it.

A rustle near the schoolhouse drew Judith's attention. She turned to see a tall, dark-haired young man, a book in his hand, walking across the school yard. "Master Simon!" a boy yelled after him, running down the stairs, "Master Simon!" The two of them stopped, conversed for a minute, and then the boy ran back inside the building while the man continued on his way. They must be letting out soon, Judith thought. And that must be William and Gilbert's new teacher, Simon Hunt.

As if sensing a pair of eyes on him Simon turned towards the tree where Judith was sitting and looked in her direction. Judith flushed with embarrassment and instinctively retreated further into the shade. She squeezed her eyes shut and prayed that Master Simon hadn't seen her, or that if he had, he would just leave it be. Judith counted the seconds slowly, a method that had always worked to calm her nerves in the past, but before she could get to five she was interrupted by the high-pitched screams of a schoolhouse of boys as they were let out of confinement for the day. She looked over her shoulder and watched as the army of small children streamed out of the building, scattering in different directions. Simon was still standing where he had been before she closed her eyes, but she was able to ignore him as she searched for her brothers, waving her arms at them before they finally spied her.

"We can walk home by ourselves," the younger Gilbert said petulantly as he joined his older sister. He made sure to stay far enough ahead that she couldn't try to walk alongside him.

"I know," Judith said. "I was just taking a walk myself. 'Tis a nice day, you know."

"'Tis hot."

Judith tried to think of what to say next when Richard Whateley rushed past them yelling, *"The youth in vain his melting pinions shakes!"*

William, suddenly alert, looked up from the ground where he'd been kicking pebbles and shouted back, *"His feathers gone, no longer air he takes!"* Turning to his sister, his eyes bright, William recited the rest of the verse:

> *Oh! Father, father, as he strove to cry,*
> *Down to the sea he tumbled from on high,*
> *And found his Fate; yet still subsists by fame,*
> *Among those watchers that retain his name.*

"It's the story of Icarus, son of Daedalus," he explained, "the boy who tries to fly with a pair of wax wings. Alas, he gets too close to the sun and the wings melt and he falls to the sea and dies."

"How sad!" Judith exclaimed.

"I suppose," William agreed. "I d'know."

"They're all like that," Gilbert interjected.

"They? What are you studying now?"

Forgetting his earlier resentment against his older sister Gilbert excitedly told her, "Ovid's Metamorphoses. It's really, really, really, really good."

"Indeed, 'tis the best book we've studied so far," William added, "not boring or dry like the others we've had to memorize. This one's about gods and mortals and curses and battles. We've already read about the four ages of man, the silver age, the bronze age, the iron age, and the gold age where man finds justice and peace. And we've read about Medea, the evil wench who betrays her husband. Tomorrow we'll get to the battle of Troy and the rise of King Caesar."

"That's quite a lot for one book," Judith admitted, trying to keep up with everything her brothers were saying.

"Master Simon tells us there's a story in there for every life experience. He told us it's his favorite book too."

"Is Master Simon your new teacher?"

"Yay, he hails from Oxford." Judith perceived a note of awe in her brother's voice. She could tell that they liked their new teacher already.

"Do you remember any more of what you learned? Can you recite more for me?"

"Of course," Gilbert boasted, and William nodded in agreement. "But shan't we be getting home?"

"Let's take the long way, past Clopton Bridge."

The boys groaned, but Judith led the way and they followed as their elder sister turned down Church Lane. William and Gilbert recited more of the Metamorphoses and the words, the phrases, were like music to Judith. She lost herself in the rhyme and meter of the poem, the emotion and the tragedy of the stories. Her thoughts whirled like a potter's wheel. When they arrived, far too soon, at the old stone bridge Judith begged a rest before they continued on their way. Both William and Gilbert knew that this was a ruse, a stalling tactic to gain time and hear more about their day, but they gave in. It had always been a mystery to them why their sister was quite so interested in their difficult daily lessons, but they loved Judith, and if she wanted to hear more about the Latin poets, they'd tell it to her. And anyways, having to recite things on the way home, Gilbert had found, only made him remember his lessons better the next day, leading to much less frequent beatings with the stick. And William enjoyed reciting the poems because it gave him a chance to imagine the characters in detail, whether the kings had dark eyes and grimacing faces as they committed their acts of murder and aggression, or whether they had clear eyes and innocent expressions, proof that they were in fact unwilling agents buffeted by the gods into horrible acts of transgression. All three Shakespeare children sat down together off the side of the bridge, their feet dangling close to the rushing water, their shoulders bumping as they talked. William and Gilbert recited more Ovid and Judith, as if in heaven, drank it in.

When the Shakespeare children finally made it home they feared getting in trouble for being gone so long. Standing just outside the front door Gilbert berated William for talking on and on about stupid King Caesar, until Judith shut him up with a pinch on the arm.

"Aye! What was that for?

"To remind you to be quiet. We don't want to upset mother for anything more than being tardy, and coming in arguing will upset her. Do you want to give her cause to forbid us going to the play?"

Gilbert shook his head.

The door creaked open and the children held their breath but for once, their mother wasn't waiting directly behind the window. They looked at each other in disbelief and breathed a sigh of relief. They could hear Joan and Anne inside the house, talking about the upcoming show.

"How many people will be there?" Anne asked, her voice thin and willowy.

Joan paused, considering the question. The girls were sitting by the hearth sewing. "The whole town, I imagine. As much as will fit in the guildhall, that's a surety."

"Do you think there'll be any royalty?"

"Royalty?" Gilbert guffawed, joining his sisters. "Of course not, why would any royalty favor Stratford?"

Anne looked down, embarrassed. She was remembering the stories their father had told them about the mystery plays in Coventry. How in previous times Henry VIII, Margaret of Anjou, Mary Tudor, and even Queen Elizabeth herself had showed up in Coventry - which was less than a day's ride away from Stratford - with a retinue of carriages and hundreds of servants and stayed to see the plays that were performed. Why couldn't that happen in Stratford? Anne would have given anything for a glimpse of the Queen and her liverymen and jewel-bedecked litter.

"Alas child, you don't want the Queen showing up in Stratford." John had been listening to his children from the doorway to the workroom, and now that he was done organizing his leather scraps into cheverel, sheepskin, calf-skin, and dog's leather, he joined them. "The last time the Queen graced Coventry for the annual mystery plays a fight broke out between the craft guilds over who would get to perform for her. The Weavers stole props from the Tailors so they couldn't put on their production, and in retaliation the Tailors poisoned the Weavers best actor, Master John, so that he was too sick to perform. Fights broke out in the pubs and the town jail was overloaded."

Anne had a hard time imagining so much commotion. She shook her head. "Will we at least get to see the Doomsday play?"

"No, the Worcester's Men aren't here to put on the biblical mystery plays," John said, picking his daughter up and sitting down with her on his lap. Which is why your mother will not be joining us, he added to himself. Mary refused to see the modern plays most troupes put on nowadays; fanciful tales about couples falling in love or families with mixed-up identities. She missed the traditional mystery plays, performed since the 14th century, which documented the biblical stories from creation to the end of the world, and which had moral lessons and teachings for the people. "They have their own plays to perform."

By the time the Shakespeare family made its way to the guildhall in the center of town the sun was well past the noon hour. Already the crowd surrounding the building was three people deep and Judith recognized many of her neighbors laughing and milling about, including Gilbert Bradley the grocer with his two sons Peter and Thomas, William Smith the haberdasher - little William's godfather and namesake - and the inseparable Symons twins, always sitting or standing together, holding hands. Pressed up against a corner window of the guildhall Judith spied Richard Whateley, sitting atop his older brother's shoulders, his hands cupped around his face, yelling to the crowd around him the news of the players as they got the stage ready to perform.

"That boy's been here since school let out," George Whateley, Richard's father, said to John Shakespeare as he slapped him on the back. "I see your family's here, even the girls."

John nodded, squeezing a half-penny into William's hand so he could go and buy a sack of sugared apples for the children to share.

"Where are Katherine and Elizabeth?" Judith asked, inquiring after Mr. Whateley's own daughters.

"At home," George paused, looking pointedly at John, "where women belong." John straightened up and smiled. He laughed, as if George had told a winning joke, and then asked how business was. George, chronically poor and unable to make a success of his unguents trade, didn't like to be reminded of the difficulties of business.

Judith scanned the crowd, noting that while there were more men in it than women, she certainly wasn't the only female there. The crowd was quite multi-faceted, including everyone from children to housewives to wealthy tradesmen. Off to the right, by the pedagogue's house, she spied a trio of sisters with their common appearance and similar hair color, arms linked together and laughing loudly. Close to the center of the crowd she saw a pair of well-dressed men, with fine plumed hats and doublets slashed with silk. They had multiple rings on their fingers which reflected the sun's bright glare as they waved their arms in animated conversation. Near the front of the crowd, huddled together against the side of the building, were a number of poor country folk dressed in homespun brown kerseys and heavy, hobnail shoes. They must have walked for miles, Judith thought, since early that morning, just to make it to the show this afternoon. Judith took in the wide mix of people and noted with satisfaction how everyone got along, how they all stood shoulder to shoulder and didn't seem to mind it.

A ripple of anticipation traveled through the crowd as the doors to the guildhall opened and a player in bright colored netherhose and bulging pleated canions called for the town council. Thomas Lucy, a fellow alderman, approached John Shakespeare. "Come man, 'tis time to take our seats." John left his children in the care of their older sister and made his way through the crowd. Just before he stepped into the guildhall he turned his head and spied Langrake across the field, his dark hair, beard, and cloak unmistakable. Even from such a distance Langrake's pointed gaze pierced John's shallow calm. He fumbled for the hilt of the dagger on his hip. Luckily, there was no way for Langrake to approach him as the crowd was too thick and, besides, the production was about to begin. John prayed that by the time the show was over, Langrake would be gone.

Judith wondered why her father paused on the threshold to the guildhall and stared into the crowd. Perhaps he was looking for them, she thought as she waved enthusiastically in his direction, but he never caught her eye. She worried that he too had noticed Anne's repeated coughing into the side of her sleeve.

"D'you have another ha'penny?" Gilbert asked, tugging on Judith's sleeve. She held out an empty, open palm. Judith smiled at her brothers and sisters, noting their sugary, wet lips. "Nay, though it doesn't matter now anyhow, we're about to go in."

The Shakespeare children ended up against the back wall of the guildhall. William, Gilbert, and Judith stood in a row with Joan and Anne nestled in front of them; Anne leaning against Judith's legs for support. A small wooden stage had been erected at the front of the guildhall, only about a foot and a half off the ground, but more than twelve feet wide. There was also a makeshift canopy over the stage, decorated with brush and brambles to suggest a sort of roof or sky cover. Judith wondered if the play was set to take place in the forest, like so many of her own were. A tree at one end of the stage leaned precariously, its branches reaching into and above the verdant canopy. As Judith watched the actors rolled out a floor of green grass to complete the marvelous setup.

When the first actor came on stage the crowd hushed instantly. The actor was a short, thick man, dressed all in white, hobbling about with the aid of a gnarled oak walking stick. He was the banished king, here to tell everyone about the downfall of his once great empire. His voice was deep and rattly and his arms swung about as he related the intrigues and battles of the first years of his reign. Judith watched his every movement, and when, at the wave of his hand, a pigeon flew up from behind the canopy, the crowd gasped and Judith's heart leaped.

Later, when the king's daughter came on stage, Judith knew the part would be played by a boy, but she found herself wishing it could have been her. She would have played the part much better, she knew it. She wouldn't have stood with such a slump, she would have spoken with much more emotion and feeling, and she certainly would have walked about the stage with much more grace. If only that could have been her!

When the evil knight tromped on stage next, half hidden by the tree and only visible at first to the audience, the crowd booed and hissed - someone even threw the butt end of a loaf of bread at him - but the actor stayed in character and managed to woo the princess to betray her father's battle plans, despite the outbursts from the audience warning her to the contrary. When the goodly king and his daughter were forced to flee the empire, Judith's heart sank and she felt betrayed by the outcome.

As the play progressed the costumes evolved in color and detail, the props became more elaborate, and the audience grew rowdier. As the minutes passed even frail Anne failed to show any obvious signs of exhaustion. She gripped Judith's legs at key moments of suspense, and tugged on her skirts for recognition of unexpected plot twists, but she did not cough and she was as engrossed as all the Shakespeare children to learn the fate of the noble, if naive, old king.

When the final act of the play began Judith wondered if the rumors they'd heard from others in the crowd could possibly be true. It was claimed that the final act included black magic; that the evil knight literally rose off of the stage and plucked audience members from the crowd and made them disappear. Judith was pretty sure that these stories couldn't possibly be true, that they were made up to excite little awed Gilbert and the other small children, but you never knew. How was the end of an empire depicted? What happened when a rich dynasty was extinguished for good?

At last the final act began with a low, ominous drumbeat. The canopy rippled, the rhythm advanced, and the crowd grew anxious. A black cloth fell from the top of the trees to the floor of the stage and between the layers a bloodied face appeared, slipping and dying in agony as cries of mercy and the screams of battle grew behind him. The crowd was mesmerized.

The evil knight fought his way on stage, face blackened with paint, clothes splattered in gore, and considered aloud the fate of the empire. In his hands he held a model globe of the world, which he squeezed and kicked about as with a toy. When a bold member of the audience broke the spell by booing loudly, the reaction was immediate. The knight dropped the globe, grabbed a leather club, and jumped into the crowd, beating at whomever didn't make way for him. When the knight found the offending audience member he grabbed him by the neck, dragged him onstage, and threw him back behind the curtain where, indeed, he was never seen again, although occasionally his screams were heard at opportune moments during the rest of the act.

The final battle scene between the old king and the young knight began as a swordfight. The two sides were evenly matched because after a few minutes of excellent swordplay, nobody had the upper hand. Then the king made a speech and the heavens replied with a clap of thunder. From somewhere atop the canopy rolls of yellow cloth were unfurled imitating the storm. The knight laughed and gave his own speech and then from the floor, this time, a burst of orange flame was directed upwards towards the king. The audience took a step back. Suddenly hail came from the canopy and rocks were thrown up from behind the tree. The battle accelerated until, in the end, the model globe of the world erupted into a ball of flame, sending both the knight and the king toppling from the stage. A cloud of smoke enveloped everything and, emerging victorious but crippled, the young knight declared victory.

Judith put a hand to her face and imagined she could feel the heat from the ball of flame on her skin. Her heart beat rapidly and her head swam with excitement from the battle. She looked around at the mesmerized audience, no one moving, barely anyone breathing, before the calls of appreciation rang out. At that moment Judith knew, that if she were a boy, she would be begging the Worcester's Men to let her join them.

3

In the dream Judith is holding a quill and scratching it hard against the surface of a scrap of paper. But no words are coming out. She has a very important play to write, a story she must get onto paper about a young noblewoman exiled from court who ends up wandering the forest dressed as a soldier...but nothing will come out of the quill. Exasperated, Judith holds the instrument up to her face, turns it around, nibbles the sharp, hard end of it, and then dips the thing back into the ink and tries again. But no matter how hard she scratches it simply won't write. Close to tears Judith tips her head back, gulps the ink in one long draught, and then throws the bottle against the wall where its thick glass shatters into a mist of dangling pieces...

Blinking rapidly in the moonlight Judith woke from her dream. She sat up and counted the seconds to calm her beating heart and realized that the scratching of the quill was just a squirrel climbing the side of the house, and the breaking of the glass was the shed door slamming in the breeze again because somebody forgot to latch it. Exhausted from these nightly writing dreams Judith rubbed her eyes, and sank back into the blankets. Her mind returned to the story from her dream.

The young woman walks alone in the forest, dressed up as a soldier, but she is eventually joined by an exiled duke... together they hatch a plan to return to town... but in the process the woman falls in love with the duke, who is unaware that the soldier he has befriended is really a beautiful young noblewoman...

Turning over in bed Judith slapped at a bug crawling up the side of her arm. The sound hung in the air.

"Judith? Are you awake?"

"Aye." Judith let out her breath. "Go back to sleep."

"No matter," Anne whispered, slipping out of bed and tiptoeing across the room. "I've been up for some time."

"Quick, get under the covers," Judith admonished. "You shouldn't be standing there in your bare feet."

Anne giggled and slipped into the pallet next to her sister. Judith's body was warm and comforting and Anne pressed her small cold feet up against her sister's enveloping heat. "Another writing dream?"

Judith nodded.

"Tell me."

Judith sighed and described for her sister the image she'd had of the beautiful young noblewoman wandering the forest alone, her long copper hair tucked up under a monmouth cap. The thick trees in full bloom. The rabbits and deer that didn't run from the sound of her step.

"But a woman can't wander the forest all by herself," Anne interrupted. "Especially not a noblewoman. That doesn't make any sense." Anne always wanted the stories to be realistic; she had a hard time with the make-believe Judith often sprinkled into her plots. "What she needs is a friend. You should have her exiled

29

into the forest, but her favorite maidservant insists on going with her."

"But she's dressed as a man, as a soldier. That's why she can do it."

"Where did she get the uniform?"

Judith paused. "But I don't want her to have help or know where she's going. I want her to get lost in the forest and have an adventure."

But Anne insisted so Judith finally agreed to a sister-like companion for the noblewoman. Together they developed the plot as the dark hours of night trickled into the early light of morning, imagining in addition a country lad that wanders the forest singing love poems, then a shepherdess who loses her way and falls into a river, and finally a reunion where everyone comes together and shares a feast. They were having so much fun imagining the story and putting the characters into all sorts of unexpected situations that Judith forgot, for just a little while, that her sister was sick. Anne's health had noticeably declined over the past two months; her cough was now a constant, there were bloody handkerchiefs strewn about the house, and while no one acknowledged it, Anne had lost her strength. She slept most of the day, finding energy only at night when she and Judith woke and talked into the early morning hours.

Every third birth shall be for the grave. Judith tried unsuccessfully to ignore the witch's prophecy that echoed in the recesses of her mind. Lately she'd taken to replacing the prophecy with words of prayer. Every Sunday at church Judith listened to the priest, seeking out some sort of clue as to what would make Anne recover, and prayed in a way she had never prayed before. Even her mother noticed, putting a kind hand on her eldest daughter's back as they walked out of church. When Judith turned, startled, her mother had smiled at her and nodded, as good a compliment as Judith had gotten in years. The last time Judith had felt this close to her mother was when her mother's sister, Aunt Joyce, had died and they'd made the trip to Warwickshire for the funeral.

Gilbert, Joan and Anne hadn't been born yet and with only Judith and William in tow, each of them sharing a horse with their mother and father, the ride had gone quickly. It had been just after Whitsuntide, when the roads were dry and free of mud and the horses fresh and eager for exercise. Judith could still remember the warmth of her mother's stomach pressed up against her back, her mother's arms encircling her protectively as she held on to the reins. The few times Judith had dared to turn her head back and look up at Mary, afraid of losing her balance on the rickety horse, she remembered her mother smiling and looking down on her reassuringly.

When they'd arrived at the large timber-framed structure in Warwickshire that was her mother's childhood home, Judith had been amazed. It seemed so big. She couldn't even count all the number of windows it had in front. Night was descending as they made their way up the drive and Judith saw that Grandma Agnes was standing outside waiting for them, her spine stiff, her arms crossed accusingly over her chest. Judith wondered how she had known the exact moment when they would arrive, or if she had been standing there, as if on guard, for hours in anticipation of their arrival. Judith had wanted to run into her grandmother's arms when she first saw her, and get a sweet treat as always happened with her Grandma Abigail, but something checked Judith's enthusiasm. No one had to tell her that things were different here. With a flat expression Grandma Agnes, before they were even off the horses, ordered Mary straight into the house, John and William around back towards the stables, and Judith to clean up her skirts where a bit of riding dust had settled. Judith looked down at the hem of her skirt, embarrassed suddenly for the dark smudges that were there, and flushed with shame. Mary lifted her daughter down from the horse, took her by the hand, and walked her swiftly into the big, dark house.

Judith had never seen such an elaborate entryway before. Large, colorful tapestries hung on the walls, real silver candlesticks stood on tall, carved wooden pedestals, and in the great hall, where her mother quickly dragged her, a perfectly clean, perfectly smooth, white linen tablecloth rested on a very long table. Mary ordered Judith to wait right there while she went to look for a rag with which to wipe the dirty skirt. Thinking she was alone, and unable to resist the perfect whiteness of it, Judith had walked over to the table and lifted a dirty finger up to touch the pristine tablecloth. Grandma Agnes, who had quietly followed them inside the house, slapped her granddaughter hard from behind. Judith burst into tears.

"Alas, what happened?" Mary asked, rushing into the room. She glanced at her daughter, then at her mother, then at her daughter again before stooping to gather the tearful child up into her arms. Mary walked Judith past her critically silent grandmother and up to the second floor. They proceeded down a long hall to a door that opened on a bed chamber sparsely furnished with a row of plain pallets and a large crucifix on the wall.

Mary sat on one of the well-worn beds and held her daughter on her lap. "'Tis my old room," she said, drying Judith's eyes and smiling at her, something she did more of in those days. Judith took in the unfamiliar surroundings.

"I shared it with my seven sisters. We all slept together, in here."

"All seven of you?" Judith asked, her eyes widening.

"All eight of us."

Judith recognized her mistake and smiled along with her mother. "There were a lot of us, that's for sure, and it was hard getting us anywhere all together. Goodness, you should have seen us in church - we took up an entire pew!" Judith and her mother giggled together.

"I wish I had seven sisters to go to church with. Then we could play games like the Whateley sisters do every week."

"You know, you aren't supposed to play games in church," Mary reminded her daughter, her tone turning serious. Judith was confused, as from her experience everybody played games in church, if they didn't fall asleep like the adults. There were only a few people, like her mother, who seemed to pay attention to things. Mary held her daughter firmly by the shoulders and looked into her eyes. "Take heed and be good on the morrow when we go to Aunt Joyce's funeral. 'Tis important, Judith. No jesting, no laughing, no falling asleep. I need you to have a noble constitution tomorrow."

Judith nodded while looking past her mother at the rest of the room. It was simple and clean, the floorboards worn from repeated scrubbings. Compared to the rest of the house it was without ornamentation. Judith turned back to her mother and was surprised to see tears welling in her eyes.

"Mother?"

"Forgive me, child," she said, wiping her cheeks with the edge of her sleeve. "I loved her," she paused to take a deep breath, "Joyce. She protected me."

Before Judith could ask what her mother meant Aunt Margaret burst into the room, hugging her sister and pinching her niece. Judith never had another moment alone with her mother for the rest of their stay, but she watched her closely through the funeral and family visit, noting how the trip wore her down. It wasn't until many years later that Judith understood why her mother was so pious, when her husband wasn't and so few of her Stratford friends were either. It was the only way she knew how to please her own stern stepmother. Agnes had been sorely disappointed when Mary had run off and married a man beneath her station, a poorer man, one who could not afford fine linen and red meat on weekdays. Only her sister Joyce had supported her. Mary had disappointed her family in her choice of husband, but she was determined to impress them with the earnestness of her piety.

On the return trip to Stratford Judith had turned in the saddle and looked at her mother, head held high on the lumbering horse, hair tied neatly in a braid twisted around her nape, and felt a pang of sadness that for some reason the family she had chosen didn't seem to be quite good enough for the family she had left. She had hugged her mother with all her strength, and at the time, her mother had hugged her back. It was the last time they'd ever been so close. Judith had tried, for awhile, to be as interested in the teachings of the Lord as her mother was, but by the time Judith turned sixteen, and had seen the fights break out between her Protestant and Catholic neighbors, and had heard of the wars that took place between England and France, and all the thousands of deaths that took place in the name of God, she had come to believe that religion was just another thing that divided people. Only now, with Anne's sickness, was Judith beginning to appreciate the role that religion could play in assuaging one's fears and, perhaps, in altering the path of fate.

"Do you ever wonder," Anne interrupted her sister's thoughts, "why we are here?"

Judith looked into her sister's eyes and shivered, despite the heat from the covers and their intertwined bodies. She shook her head.

"I think we're here," Anne offered after a minute's speculation, "in order to appreciate the things of this earth. Warm bread. A hot sun. Fresh flowers."

"Yes," Judith agreed, remembering something Father Style had said in church the week before. "God wants us to appreciate his bounty, and to strive every day to better ourselves, to help our neighbors, to work to accomplish good things."

Anne struggled to sit up against the straw tick. "No. I don't think the point is to work hard and create things, not god's things, I think the point is to slow down and enjoy things, like nature. To pay attention to the trees and brooks and stones, and the good that is in everything."

Judith nodded, wanting to agree with her sister but not certain she was understanding her. She noted again her sister's pink cheeks, flushed not with health but with fever. Judith couldn't help but wonder why her sister Anne had gotten sick, of all people. She was such a good person, and there were certainly less worthy people Judith could think of that deserved to get sick more than her, like gruff Mr. Newsham, who everyone knew drank too much and stole from the collection plate on Sundays. Judith felt again as though she were facing the deep, dark, bottomless well that she had first imagined as a child many years ago. Down that well, somewhere near the very bottom, were hell, death, meanness, starvation, and every other one of life's unknowables that she could never seem to shine a light on. All the readings William and Gilbert shared with her, from Seneca to Aristotle to Ovid helped, but even they seemed to stall before life's biggest questions. Judith squeezed her sister's hand and listened as the words and thoughts tumbled out of Anne's delicate lips.

"Did you hear that?" Judith interrupted, turning her head. Anne quieted and they listened as a soft, rustling sound drifted in through the window. Instinctively Judith and Anne rolled up their sleeves and inspected their arms for marks; everyone knew that fairies came at night and left bruises on the arms of little girls. But their skin was smooth and besides, it was nearly morning, too late for the fairies which preferred to wreak havoc earlier in the night.

"Methinks someone is outside," Judith whispered, lifting the blanket from the bed. The girls tiptoed over to the window and peered into the garden below. A dark, squat figure roamed amongst the vegetables, first standing by the cabbage, then wandering towards the tomatoes. Judith and Anne held their breaths and watched as the mysterious figure stopped, knelt down, and buried its face in the ground.

"Pray, who is that?"

"*What* is that?"

It occurred to Judith, as the figure stayed bent over and made odd scratching sounds, that if mother found the tomato bushes in disarray in the morning, it was she that would get into trouble. "Move not," Judith ordered. "I'll find out what is going on."

Judith glided down the stairs and made her way out the back door. It was still dark outside when she emerged into the cool night air, but morning was coming and early streaks of light were just creeping over the far hedges and low-lying hills. A raven flew past, crowing loudly enough to make Judith jump.

"Alas, that is a bad sign."

Judith turned and saw Anne behind her in the doorway. "I told you to stay inside."

Anne ignored this and rushed to her sister's side. Together they crept over to the vegetable garden.

As they approached the dark figure, still bent over and now making retching sounds, Judith and Anne at last recognized their mother. Judith stopped in surprise, but Anne ran past her and fell over into the dirt next to Mary.

"Mother, mother, are you ill? What 'tis it?" Anne asked, suddenly sobbing.

Mary sat up and turned towards her daughters. The look of surprise on her face gave way to weariness. She smiled at Anne and wiped her mouth.

"I'm fine, child. I'm perfectly alright. Why are you crying so?" Mary reached over to comfort her youngest daughter, but Anne pulled away.

"Are you ill?" Anne bit out between sobs. "Like me?" Finding her mother out in the garden like this, at such an ungracious hour, did not bode well and fear hit Anne like a blow. She'd told no one, but lately she'd been having dreams that the sickness nestled inside her was growing into a large and destructive monster that attacked her family as well. Now, it seemed, this very nightmare had indeed happened. Anne felt she had passed the badness and pain growing inside her onto her mother, and now they both were in trouble.

Mary looked from one daughter to the other, trying to decide what to say. She thought about all the excuses she and John had made up to tell the children if something like this came up, but suddenly they no longer seemed plausible. "'Tis no need to worry," she said to her daughters, kindly taking Anne's hand into her own. "In truth, God has blessed us yet again." Mary took a deep breath. "I am with child."

It took a moment for Anne to understand, but when she did relief spread across her face like a brightening sun. Judith smiled too and congratulated her mother. Mary seemed glad that she had told them.

"'Tis a boy or a girl?" Anne asked.

"Only God knows, but I think 'tis a boy. Only boys make me this sick." She grinned then and Anne scrambled into her arms. Mary looked at Judith over her younger daughter's shoulders and they both seemed to have the same thought at the same time. *Every third birth shall be for the grave.* The newborn would make six. If the prophecy were to hold true, it would mean that two of Mary's other children would have to die.

Judith looked down and Mary looked away. Anne coughed. Extracting herself from her mother's embrace and leaning over in a position much like the one they'd just found Mary in, Anne continued coughing until blood trickled from the side of her mouth. Judith fell on the ground next to her sister and rubbed her on the back. All three women knelt together in the cool, pungent soil as the raven flew back overhead, crowing to the early morning light.

4

"Obey your mother while I'm gone," John reminded his eldest daughter. He yanked the cinch on the horse's saddle and handed the reins to Judith. She nodded while petting the gelding on the nose and flank. John made to mount the horse but Judith stopped him.

"The gloves."

John disappeared into the shed and returned with a pair of embroidered calfskin gauntlets. They were the excuse for the trip to Coventry, how could he forget? John stuffed them into his saddlebag and smiled at his daughter. He was feeling more relaxed now that he had paid his debt to Langrake and didn't have to look over his shoulder every time he rode down Market Street. John had heard all sorts of stories about Langrake breaking the legs or cutting off the fingers of those who didn't repay their debts; he'd even heard that Langrake owned a Boot, like the one in the Tower of London, which he reserved for torturing the worst offenders. John shuddered at the thought of the bone crushing device. Thank heavens Edward had, in the end, loaned him enough money to pay off Langrake. Now all he needed was a few more profitable wool trades and he'd come out even.

John glanced overhead at the gathering clouds. It was going to rain that afternoon and he needed to get going while the roads were still dry. He hated riding in bad weather, although, a spot of rain did tend to keep the bandits away. The clouds over Stratford were dark, but further north it seemed as though things broke up a bit.

John was looking forward to this trip, to seeing his old friends at the Lion and spending a few nights at the pub without worrying about having to find his way home. His only hesitation had been his wife's condition. It seemed unlucky, somehow, to leave while Mary was with child, as if his staying could offer protection from the black magic that sometimes crept into their lives. But John pushed the thought from his mind. He had to go. He stepped onto the worn mounting stone and swung his leg over the horse. He'd be sure to ride through Lapworth on the way back and buy Mary some of that lace she loved so much. Alderman Lucy had urged him to ride through Lapworth anyway to inspect the lands, telling him that tithes could be had for a good price in those parts and that a sound tithe was more than a business prospect, it was certain income for the long run.

Judith handed her father the reins, silently wishing she could accompany him to Coventry. She'd always wanted to travel, to see something other than Stratford, even if it was only a neighboring town. Were the streets as wide there? The cottages as tall? But Judith kept her thoughts to herself, knowing it would be foolish to broach such a subject. She leaned her head against the good-natured horse and patted again its soft, wet nose.

"Here," John said, handing his daughter two half-pennys. "Buy some hair ribbon, or a treat the next time you're on Market Street." Judith closed her palm around the offering, hard and cool like stones from the river, and thanked her father. "And remember to obey your mother."

Judith watched as her father rode off, the horse kicking up clumpfuls of dirt, the saddlebag flapping in rhythm with the beast's stride, the disappearing figure drawing something out of her, as a pulled string draws out the work of a stitch. The wind was picking up, whipping Judith's kirtle high around her ankles. She held her skirts tightly at her sides and made her way back inside the house.

It was calm indoors, a little dim even with the encroaching darkness outside. Judith made her way up the stairs and checked on Anne, still sleeping under the pile of blankets that seemed to grow around her every day. Judith brushed the hair from Anne's forehead, rearranged the pillows, and set out a fresh hand towel by her bed. After a time, she went back downstairs.

"Stealing apples again!"

The sound of Mrs. Whateley's voice drew Judith to the hearth where she found her mother resting from her work, talking with their neighbor. Mrs. Whateley nodded to Judith as she joined them. "There was a knock on the door and when I opened it who was there, but farmer Biddle! Holding little Richard by the ear. He told me to keep my bairns off his land and away from his barrel - you know, the one behind the barn, topped with rotting apples. By my life, 'twas hard to keep from laughing. I assured the good farmer that it wouldn't happen again, and I twisted Richard's arm hard. Scolded the boy good and made him promise never to do it again," Mrs. Whateley nodded. "But ye know he will," she added, almost proudly.

"Why does Richard keep stealing *rotten* apples?"

Mrs. Whateley shrugged. "He says they taste good."

The older women looked at each other and laughed.

"You have your hands full with that one," Mary teased her friend.

"'Tis true," Mrs. Whateley agreed. "Boys are a world of trouble. I don't wish another one on you, although," she added, glancing at Judith but talking as if she weren't there, "girls aren't much easier."

Judith colored slightly and looked away. "Shall I peel the potatoes?" she asked.

"Nay. Work on your stitching this afternoon. It won't be long before this baby arrives, and we need more clothes. Get the boys' old linen from the trunk, those shirts they grew out of last year. We'll start with those and make a few more shifts for the baby. After you've cut the pattern make sure Joan embroideries the hems. You sister is quite good with the needle and I trust her to make flowered hems for the baby."

Judith turned to go. "And while you've opened the trunk," Mary called out, "find the boys' old hornbook. We'll need it if this is another boy and I looked everywhere earlier but couldn't find it."

Judith stood very still and tried to look unaffected. She knew where the hornbook had gone; she'd used it a couple of years ago to learn the alphabet and it was likely still in her bed chamber, hidden behind the bedstead where it'd sat for years. Judith wondered how she could surreptitiously retrieve it without alerting her mother.

"'Tis another thing with boys," Mrs. Whateley added, "they're always losing things! Or destroying things. I can't keep a pair of shoes on my boys for the world. They tear 'em to shreds running through the forest and climbing trees before we can ever afford to buy new ones. I've had Richard's startups restitched so many times now 'tis a wonder they hold together at all."

Judith slipped upstairs as Mrs. Whateley related her story, tiptoeing as quietly as she could into her own bed chamber, rather than the boys'. She made sure Anne was still asleep before mounting her pallet, reaching back behind the headboard, and feeling for the hornbook. But her arm was too big. It no longer fit behind the bed like it used to and Judith could just touch, but not grab, the illusive item. She was sweating by the time Joan walked into the room.

"What are you doing?"

Judith yanked her arm from behind the headboard and it caught painfully. She gave Joan an annoyed look.

"What are you *doing*?"

"Shhhh." Judith held her finger to her lips and got off the bed. She grabbed her sister's arm and walked the two of them out of the room. She was going to have to get the hornbook later, when it was safer.

The sky was still gray and overcast later that afternoon when it was time for the boys to come home from school. Judith had so far been unable to return to the bed chamber and retrieve the hornbook without anyone noticing, so she needed to warn her brothers before they came home that their mother was looking for it. William and Gilbert knew where the hornbook was since they'd given it to Judith two summers past when she'd begged them for help learning her letters. They'd never really been happy about giving her the learning tool, but at the time they'd been more easily persuaded by her elder authority. Since then Gilbert had grown more independent and Judith feared that if he were confronted he would simply relent to save his hide and reveal his sister's illicit schooling activities. Judith had to get to her brothers first.

After sticking her head out the window to confirm the inauspicious weather, Judith told her mother that she was stepping outside to gather the tools from the garden before it started raining. Her mother nodded, unconcerned, and when Judith was safely out of the house she turned and snuck down Henley Street. When she got to the corner of Henley and Church she crossed her fingers, hopped on her left foot three times, and made a wish to the fairies to keep the rain away till evening.

The ground around the tree where she often waited for her brothers was, luckily, still dry. Careful not to dirty her skirts too much Judith sat down, leaned against the tree, and closed her eyes. The worried purpose of her visit slipped from her mind as she fell into a daydream. She imagined herself in rich costume, a dress of purple velvet, pearls studded in her hair, brocade slippers in gold and silver design, sweeping across a stage projecting her voice to an audience that expanded out as far as the eye could see. Whole towns had made the trip to see her play and watch her act. She was the Queen of France...a mysterious moor...a beautiful courtier in love with a prince. Yes, that was it, Judith was a lowly courtier who had gained her court appointment through luck and hard work and who, once there, worked to gain the favor of the royal family through her wit and intelligence. Yes, yes, and when the noble prince returned from his travels and saw her in the hall for the first time, he-

"Pardon me, is this yours?"

Judith's eyes flew open and she saw before her Master Hunt, the boys' teacher, glancing down with a smile on his lips, a yellow daisy extended in his hand. Abruptly Judith stood up, fumbling and keeping her eyes downcast. Simon tried again to give her the flower, but she avoided acknowledging it and kept her hands behind her back, against the tree for support.

"I've seen you here before, waiting for the Shakespeare boys is it?"

Judith nodded.

"They are worthy students. It surprises me they need help finding their way home."

Judith glanced up and saw that Master Simon was making a joke. The knot in her throat eased somewhat.

"Pray tell me, why do you accompany William and Gilbert so often? Do they not make their way home as they should? I can speak with them, if you'd like."

"No, no," Judith rushed to answer. She didn't want to get William or Gilbert in any sort of trouble, "'tis nothing like that. As you say, they are good boys."

"Well I'm certain you don't take the trouble for mine own sake," Simon coughed, clearing his throat, "though I might wish it so."

Judith lifted her head and glanced up at Master Hunt. Carefully, he slid the yellow daisy into the front of her bodice. Judith's chest pounded and she felt light headed. She'd never been this nervous in front of anyone before.

"'Tis just that, well, I favor walking the boys home," Judith managed to get out. "We talk."

"You talk?" Many times Simon had noticed this beautiful girl waiting outside his classroom at the end of the day, and many times he'd imagined what it would be like to go up to her, but something had always held him back. "About what?"

"I-, well-, we-, tell stories." It sounded dumb. Judith hadn't meant to say that, but she couldn't very well tell Master Simon that William and Gilbert were her teachers, and that they were about to get into trouble for a misplaced hornbook. She couldn't tell him how she was often down there after school begging her little brothers to recite Latin and pass on their daily lessons. Before she had time to think about it, she'd somehow blurted out that they made up 'stories'. How stupid could she be?

"Stories?" Simon asked with genuine surprise. "What kind of stories?"

Judith's mind raced to come up with something, to try and salvage the situation and say something smart, yet appropriate, and at the same time something that wouldn't earn her brothers a beating with the stick. She felt the first drop of rain on her neck as the sky darkened considerably.

"Did William see the Worcester's Men when they came through town?"

Judith nodded. The rain increased.

Suddenly Simon grabbed Judith's hand. "Quick! We need cover." He dragged her across the grass to an old shed behind the pedagogue's house. It was dark and dank inside, and Judith couldn't make much out besides some farming tools, an old horse collar, and a row of barrels. For a minute, they just stood inside the doorway and watched as the rain came down in sheets.

"And Gilbert too."

Simon looked at her questioningly.

"Gilbert saw the players too, not just William."

He smiled. "They're lucky boys then. Not everyone had the chance to see the Worcester's Men. I wish I'd had, but I couldn't get inside the guildhall."

"Oh, they were wonderful, better than anything you might have heard."

"You were there?" Simon asked, his eyes widening.

"Yes, our whole family was." Judith forgot for a moment her mother's absence.

Simon took in Judith's clear blue eyes, her tall frame, and her shining blond hair. It would have been unthinkable, where he grew up, for a young maiden to go and see a players' show. The way his father described it, plays were no longer good biblical teachings but rowdy, disorderly affairs that attracted the lowest elements of society and encouraged poor behavior.

In the half-light Judith couldn't read the expression on Simon's face. The fact that he wasn't saying anything all of a sudden made her nervous, so she blurted out a stream of words. "We stood at the back of the guildhall, along the wall. We had a goodly view of the stage. It was beautiful, with a carpet of grass, trees, even a canopy. The performance was breathtaking, the costumes and the acting." Judith waited for Simon to interrupt her, but he didn't. "You should have seen the audience, riveted to the stage. The knight was as outrageous as Herod, stomping about and brandishing his sword, yelling his lines at the audience..."

If Judith went to the plays, Simon thought, and if she was this uninhibited and talkative, then surely she was familiar with the ways of the world. Simon couldn't believe his luck, finding in Stratford such a beautiful young girl who was also so open, approachable, and garrulous. He took a step towards her, and she didn't take a step back.

"Did you know that the Queen went to the mystery plays in Coventry a few years back? And when she left she donated half her clothes to the actors for future performances?"

In the half-light from the doorway Judith's profile was illuminated. Simon couldn't help thinking that her skin was perfect. "Nay, I did not know that."

"Yay, everything, skirts, shoes, gloves, even hair pieces. My brothers and sisters and I want to build our own stage, maybe out in the woods." Judith blushed, realizing that she'd said too much, but for some reason, she couldn't stop herself. Master Hunt seemed genuinely interested in what she had to say and no one, besides her little siblings, had ever been that interested before.

Simon smiled at Judith. In the moist, dark atmosphere of the shed he could smell her scent. He hadn't been with a woman since Oxford, since the graduation celebration when he and his classmates had finally gotten shy Tommy Bairns to an alehouse and then a brothel for the first time. He'd yearned for the feel of a woman since then, but hadn't known where to go in this small town, and he didn't want to draw attention to himself. He took another step closer to Judith and glanced down at the soft curve of her breasts as they disappeared beneath the thin white material of her bodice. "What was your favorite part of the show?"

"My favorite part?" Judith stopped to think. She looked outside and wondered when the boys would be let out of the school house. They must be waiting for the rain to stop as well. She looked back at Master Hunt, going through the play again in her head, when she suddenly lost her train of thought. He had a funny expression on his face which drove a sliver of fear into her heart. She tried to move away, but bumped into something behind her and stumbled. Simon reached out and caught her.

Holding her in his arms, feeling her warm body pressed up against his, Simon couldn't help himself. With a rough movement he jerked Judith's head up to his.

The hot, stuffy atmosphere of the shed clouded Judith's senses and made it hard for her to focus. The last thing she knew she was talking about the play, and then it seemed Simon's arms were around her and he was forcing his wet lips against hers. What was happening? The shed was suffocating. Judith struggled against Master Hunt and tried to regain her balance.

But Simon only grew more insistent as he felt Judith move beneath him. He stuck his tongue into her mouth and didn't notice when she didn't kiss back. The kind of women Simon had been with rarely kissed back, and he'd always assumed women just liked it that way. His father had told him many times that women liked to play coy. Simon's grip on Judith tightened and his fingers bit into her flesh.

The pain of Master Hunt's wrenching grip shocked Judith awake. She struggled more determinedly, but was surprised to find out how strong Master Hunt really was. She cried out, but he ignored her, and her voice only got lost in the shadows of the shed. When she kicked Master Hunt in the knees he let out a grunt of pain and for a moment his grip loosened, before he fell on top of her, bringing both of them down onto the ground. His long, heavy frame pinned Judith to the dirt as tears sprang to her eyes.

Simon felt alive, as if the world were there for his taking. Pleasure was his, pain was a distant memory, and nothing was meant to stop him. He deserved this. He deserved this small pleasure after how hard he worked all day, every day, for those bothersome little runts. And clearly she liked it too. Simon joined in Judith's struggling game and happily pinned her arms behind her head. He couldn't help but get excited by their small struggle, by Judith's perfectly round white breasts, by her beautiful long neck exposed and taut. He pressed himself hard against her, oblivious to the tears that streamed from her eyes.

The shame of what was happening overpowered Judith. Master Simon hadn't been interested in what she'd had to say, she realized now, he'd only been interested in her sex. This was what her mother had been telling her to be careful of, for years now. She struggled hard beneath Simon's weight but she was struggling at the same time to keep the tears and embarrassment away. She heard a rip and knew that her shift had been torn. Closing her eyes Judith tried to think of anything other than what was happening; she tried to remember the joy of the play, she had an image of talking and giggling next to sweet innocent Anne, what did she say? All that mattered was fresh bread, pretty flowers, a warm sun. As Master Hunt's thick hand moved up along her slim thigh she pretended none of it was happening, that she was far away on a ship at sea, traveling the oceans like she sometimes did in her dreams. When he entered her with a violent thrust, Judith bit down on her tongue and drew blood.

When it was all over, Judith stared fixedly at the horse collar in the corner while Simon tidied his clothes and walked out of the shed without a word. Judith continued to lay there and listen to the rain coming down. She remembered how, as a child, the plink-plop of raindrops landing on the roof of the house used to comfort her and help her fall asleep. She'd always liked imagining all the flowers and all the trees of the world finally getting their long-awaited drink. For the first time, however, the sound of the rain didn't comfort her at all.

When Judith finally stood up it stung between her legs and every step she took stabbed like a dagger. A sticky substance ran down her legs, but she was too numb to check and see if it was blood or something else. She slipped out of the shed and walked towards home, not waiting for her brothers, not looking to see who was around, not wanting, in fact, to talk to anyone at all. All she wanted was to get home. As she walked her small tears mingled with the large raindrops overhead. She replayed the events by the tree in her head, searching for some sign of what she had done wrong. What she had done to make Master Hunt act as he did. Master Hunt was a teacher, an educated man, she knew he wouldn't have done what he did if she hadn't given him the wrong sign.

Half way down Church Street Judith stumbled and fell, bruising her knees and palms. Wet mud from the road clung to her skirt and hair. For a minute she simply sat there, dumbfounded. Then she gathered herself together, got up, and made it the rest of the way home.

Her mother was standing in the doorway, looking out into the rain.

"Went to fetch your brothers? I can't imagine they're walking home in this rain. They're probably waiting it out in the school house."

Judith looked at the face she'd known since she was a child, at the lips that used to kiss her forehead and give her kind words, at the eyes that used to crinkle in delight when she was much, much smaller. She thought about putting her head on her mother's chest, about trying to crawl into her mother's embrace. She yearned for any small affection.

"Are you crying, child? Whatever is the matter?"

At this, Judith's tears poured unabated.

"Come into the house child, come here." Mary sat Judith down by the hearth and asked what had happened. Judith, for the first time, was at a loss for words. She wanted to tell her mother everything, she was desperate to relate the horror of the afternoon and so, with words, shape it, construct it, and ultimately get it off her chest, but she had a feeling deep in the pit of her stomach that her mother would not react well to the story. Judith hesitated, and her mother grew impatient.

"For goodness sake's, child, tell me what's the matter, or forget about it and be done, but stop just sitting there looking like the shadow of the moon."

Haltingly, Judith related the story of Master Simon and the shed, but as she described the events, she watched her mother stiffen. She wondered if maybe she shouldn't have been quite so candid. Having to tell the story had at least made her stop crying.

"How could you have been so stupid?" her mother finally asked, standing up and walking across the room.

It felt like another blow.

"Have I not been telling you to be careful? Have I not been warning you that something like this could happen?"

"I'm sorry, mother. I- I guess I never understood. You always told me to be careful with Uncle Edward, that he doesn't play right with girls...but..." And suddenly Judith did understand - perfectly. Her mother had never liked returning to Warwickshire and the farmstead where she grew up, where now only her brother Edward still remained, not because her stepmother had been so strict, not because the memory of Aunt Joyce had been too painful, but because Edward had taken advantage of her, at some point in the past, and now she tried to avoid him. Judith recalled seeing Uncle Edward, that time they had gone back for Aunt Joyce's funeral, grab her mother's hand and try to talk to her out in the garden, and she had thought it odd when her mother had quickly pulled away and left. But now, it all made sense.

"This is your fault, Judith, for getting into such a situation. Why did you go into a shed with him alone?"

"It- It was raining."

"I know not what we are going to do. Simon Hunt is a respected man in this town. He's educated, he went to Oxford. He's the boys' teacher." Her mother paced back and forth. "What's done cannot be undone," she mumbled, before turning and asking, "When did you last bleed?"

Judith's head was swimming but she tried to focus her thoughts. "A week ago, I think."

"Hm. We'll have to wait and see." Mary resumed her pacing.

Judith shivered and wrapped her arms tightly around herself; her wet clothes clung heavily to her body. Images of Master Hunt's hungry eyes wouldn't leave her mind.

"You are never allowed to go back to that school house again," Mary told Judith pointedly. "Do you understand me?"

Judith nodded, her heartbreak complete. All her lessons with William and Gilbert, the thing she most looked forward to, everything, ruined.

"Do you understand me?" Mary repeated.

"Yes, mother."

Suddenly there was a loud crash from somewhere up above their heads. Judith and her mother glanced at each other before rushing up the stairs and heading for the girl's bed chamber. They found Anne in a heap on the floor, a rag doll with the life washed out of her. The sleeves of her gown were red with blood and in her hand was gripped a crimson, sopping handkerchief. Mary fell to her knees and grabbed her daughter. She shook Anne by the shoulders and called out her name. Joan rushed into the room then, but stopped just past the threshold as she took in the scene before her, her hand covering her mouth in horror. Judith backed out of the way and huddled against the far wall, away from poor, sweet, innocent Anne. Judith was shivering so badly her teeth clicked and her head jerked on her neck. Nothing made any sense anymore. Why would God take Anne; she wasn't the bad one. Judith stared uncomprehendingly straight ahead as Joan kneeled beside her mother, comforting her as she comforted little Anne's small, lifeless body.

5

After Anne's death a stillness settled over the Shakespeare household. Mary shuffled her feet and tarried over her sewing, losing herself in thought over single stitches. John cloistered himself in the workroom and spoke to no one, irritated by even small interruptions for food or drink. Gilbert, noting the lack of supervision, made himself scarce, playing outside with Richard Whateley or the Bradley boys every evening until dark. Joan, unmoored by the sadness that drifted through the house, tried to steady the void of her sister's absence with quiet chatter that no one paid much attention to. And Judith, unable for the first time to cheer herself with stories of make-believe imagined in her head, sat quietly by the hearth as the days dripped past. She had smiled gratefully when her bleeds had come, and immediately shared the news with her mother, but when Mary didn't seem any happier for it Judith too remained downcast. Only William maintained any sense of equilibrium in the weeks succeeding Anne's death. It was William who made sure when he got home from school that the animals were fed and the garden tended. It was William who cleaned up after supper. And it was William who tried, one Sunday six weeks after Anne's death, to get his siblings back into their old routine.

"What say we gather the props and go out to the forest?"

Judith glanced at her brother as she hung her cloak on a peg by the front door. Gilbert and Joan paused.

"Soon winter will be upon us and then it'll be too cold to play outside."

But Gilbert only shrugged and Judith and Joan, without a word, followed him upstairs to change out of their Sunday best. Disappointed, William sat in front of the hearth. After a restless moment he picked up the family bible and flipped through it for something to read. When Judith reentered the hall a few minutes later in her familiar brown kirtle and white workaday apron, William called out to her. "Shall I read a passage?"

Judith nodded and went to sit by her brother. William continued aloud the passage he'd been reading from the Book of Luke, but after awhile he looked up and saw that his sister's attention had wandered. He cleared his throat and asked the question he'd been wanting to ask for weeks.

"Why don't you meet us at the schoolhouse anymore?"

Judith started and looked at her brother. Her face flushed slightly as she smoothed her apron across her lap. "You're old enough to walk home by yourself now. You know the way."

William was silent. Showing them the way home was a ruse, the excuse that Judith, William, and Gilbert told everyone else for why Judith sometimes showed up at the schoolhouse and walked them home; it was never a reason they'd give to one another. He tried again.

"Would you like to hear the proverbs we learned in school?" William began reciting the Latin, but it didn't take long before he could tell that, again, Judith wasn't really listening. The proof came when she failed to ask a single question, or request him to repeat a single one of the phrases, when he was done. His heart sank and he knew for certain that something had changed with his beloved older sister. He wouldn't have thought that Anne's death would have affected Judith this much, but as his teacher Master Hunt once said, there was little logic to the humors of women.

Later that afternoon Richard Whateley and his mother surprised the Shakespeare's with a visit. Judith, Joan and William were sitting in the hall, the girls sewing and William reading, when the back door opened and Richard poked his head inside.

"We come bearing gifts," Mrs. Whateley called out, pushing her son along and holding out a basket of rosemary, cloves, and sweet-scented nosegays.

Joan went to fetch her mother while Judith and William made room for the Whateleys on the bench beside the hearth.

"I gathered them this morning," Richard said, indicating the colorful blossoms in the basket.

"The rosemary is for the mind," Mrs. Whateley added. "It mostly aids in memory, but it can also make you forget." Mrs. Whateley waved handfuls of the herbs in front of her. "The cloves and the flowers are to clear the air."

Joan reentered the room with her mother.

"As I was saying," Mrs. Whateley continued, "the air in this house needs clearing. The death of a child is an awful thing, to be sure, but at a certain point one needs to move on." Mrs. Whateley stood up and walked around the room depositing nosegays and cloves in various corners of the room. "The fairies do not favor an idle house. It's time to open things up and bring in some fresh scents." When she was satisfied with her work Mrs. Whateley settled back down by the hearth. "'Tis a start."

Richard, who'd been watching Judith the whole time, couldn't restrain himself any longer. "I found something the other day," he said, reaching under his jerkin and pulling from beneath its folds a long, rusted metal rod. "Methinks it whould make a good prop." Flecks of dirt fell from the object's square sides. "'Tis a spoke, from an old wagon wheel. 'Twas buried in the ground over by the road to Shottery. It's near luck I even saw it after the rains the other day." He stopped speaking and looked at Judith for approval.

William reached over and took hold of the item. "Maybe we can use it as a wand."

Mrs. Whateley clicked her tongue. "Nay, pretend not over the magical arts."

Richard wondered why Judith remained silent. She always knew what to say, but for some reason, she wasn't saying anything.

"Put that filthy thing away," Mrs. Whateley said, clipping her son on the ear. "The ideas you get." Richard rubbed the side of his head. He couldn't understand why Judith wasn't interested in the rod; he'd been sure she'd be excited by what he'd found for her.

Mrs. Whateley turned the conversation to Mary. "How are you feeling today, dear?" She glanced at Mary's round stomach, but for the first time, didn't touch it.

"Fine," Mary smiled slightly. "In sooth, I am fine." Mary had to admit, and it was surprising even to herself, that she was in fact feeling rather healthy. The stomach sickness had passed, her odd food cravings had gone away, and so far this had been the easiest pregnancy she'd yet encountered. She kept waiting for her hips to ache and her ankles to swell, or god forbid, for the child inside her to stop kicking and grow heavy, but nothing of the kind had so far happened. Instead, it was just the opposite. She could tell that the child inside her was strong and growing and Mary felt unconscionably ruddy too.

"Now is a very important time," Mrs. Whateley said authoritatively. "After the sixth month, when the child's form begins to show, is when the dear thing is most vulnerable to witches spells and changeling's incantations. You must be especially careful right now," she said, looking earnestly at Mary. "And I know you won't want to hear this, but now is the time to rid the house of the dead child's things."

Judith sucked in her breath at the same time as she realized that Mrs. Whateley refused to say Anne's name out loud.

"I'll not suffer an argument. I'm here to help," Mrs. Whateley continued. "Richard, William, you boys go play outside. Joan, Judith, put aside your hoops. It's time we go upstairs and do what needs to be done."

Judith should have known, of course, that they'd find the hornbook. She should have stopped them as they walked single file towards the bed chamber, the weight of her dread growing. But she didn't. In all the commotion of the last few weeks, after the encounter with Master Hunt and little Anne's death, the hornbook had simply slipped from her mind. And now there was nothing she could do. When indeed the hornbook clattered to the floor during Mrs. Whateley's aggressive cleaning of the room Judith should have tried to intercept it, or come up with some excuse for its presence behind her headboard, but instead she just stood there. She was resigned to what fate seemed to be delivering.

Mary looked from the hornbook to her daughter and back again, and as realization dawned she asked softly, "Know you your letters?"

Judith nodded and a long-taut spring snapped in Mary.

"Useless child! Why do you do such things? Why do you insist on Latin and letters and stories of make-believe played in the forest? It's inappropriate! 'Tisn't right. You-" She advanced a step towards Judith, her fists clenched. "You put the boys up to this, didn't you? You stole the hornbook from them, to add to your list of sins." Mary's eyes widened in understanding. "Asips, Asops, whatever it was called, that book of fables that disappeared last year, was that you too?"

Judith felt a sting of pleasure in righting this wrong at least. "Yay. It fell into the Avon. 'Twas entirely my fault."

"This- it's-" The words stumbled together as Mary fought to straighten them out. "'Tis awful. 'Tis wrong. 'Tis against the natural order of things. Why must you insist on putting on such airs?" Mary turned and held her hands up to the rafters. She took a deep breath and declared, "It is true, there is an evil presence in this house."

Judith felt a chill run up her spine. In spite of herself, she defended her actions. "Nuns can read."

Mary turned to look at her daughter. "What are you going to do," she asked, "run off and join a nunnery?"

Judith didn't answer and Mary crossed herself.

"You don't join a nunnery to read, child, you join because you love god."

At that moment Judith desperately wished that she loved god as much as her mother did. Maybe then everything would be easier. Maybe then what she was supposed to do would be clear, her mixed up thoughts and mixed up desires would make sense.

Judith wasn't trying to upset her mother, she didn't want to be a bad daughter, she just couldn't help being who she was. She just couldn't help wanting to read.

"I need some air," Mary said, leaving the room and everything in it behind her.

John remained in his workroom through all the commotion, fashioning a pair of duello gloves for alderman Lucy. He'd heard the raised voices, the scraping of furniture, the stamping of angry feet, but had ignored it all. He couldn't be drawn into whatever it was that was going on. Not now. What he needed now was time to figure out what he was going to do about the Grand Commission. He had a fair bit of coin. After paying off Langrake he'd indeed made a few trades of his own, without any help from Edward, and they'd turned a bit of a profit. For once money wasn't the problem, this time it was the religious authorities.

Last week Robert Persons had been arrested near Rowington and there were rumors that he'd cracked under interrogation and offered the names of the Shakespeares, the Wheelers, the Debdales, and other sympathetic Catholic families around Stratford. John actually didn't know Persons well, he'd been out of town when the man passed through Stratford the year before, but Mary had given him a night's shelter. And when Persons had stayed in their house he'd left behind a testament of faith which Mary had later begged John to sign. In truth, John didn't care much about the differences between the Protestants and the Catholics, at least not as much as other people seemed to. He would never admit it to his wife, but he didn't care which queen ruled England, Mary or Elizabeth, they both ruled from a distant throne in London, their councilors both just wanted rich taxes and obsequious favors. It made no difference. Why get involved? John could kick himself for having signed that stupid testament of faith at his wife's urging. And afterwards he'd let her take it and hide it somewhere - but where? If it ended up in the wrong hands he'd be in great trouble; worse trouble than any brogging deal gone bad.

John straightened his back and rubbed his neck. His eyes hurt and there was a throbbing at the back of his skull. He recalled his last trip to Warwick and the sight of the thieves hanging from the gibbets in the center of town. Their faces were purple and swollen and their eyes had been pecked out by birds. John had wondered how long the bodies would stay up there; if someone would have mercy and take the rotting flesh down. The stench had been enough to make him lose his breakfast.

Then John thought about Anne, sweet dear peaceful Anne who was the image of heaven itself in her white shroud and floral chaplet. The floorboard creaked and Mary walked apologetically into the room.

"Husband," she said, not making direct eye contact. "Have you a moment?"

Judith thought that after six long weeks and no mention made of the incident, her mother had put aside the entire episode with Master Hunt. At first Judith had been hurt by her mother's heavy silence, but after awhile she'd succumbed to it and assumed it was for the best. Filing the episode away in some dark corner of the mind and getting on with the daily chores of life was only practical, really. Judith never imagined that her mother had held on to the horror, biding time until she could figure out what to do with it.

When Judith was called into the workroom at her mother's bidding, she knew instantly that the reckoning had arrived. The air was still, taut, like the expectant calm that hovers before a storm. She took in her mother's rigid stance, her lips pressed together, her hands clasped firmly in front of her. Judith's father, standing beside his wife but slightly apart, looked shrunken, like a withered squash fallen from the vine. His shoulders sagged, his face was sallow, and his eyes remained downcast as if he couldn't bear to look at his eldest daughter.

"It's been decided," Mary announced, "that you are to start your apprenticeship a year early."

"My apprenticeship?"

"We've arranged a position for you with the Mountjoys' in London. You'll act as maidservant to the wealthy Mrs. Mountjoy." Mary paused briefly to catch and hold her daughter's eye. "'Tis a worthy position. And they are doing us a favor by taking you early, so you needs be on your best behavior. Do you understand?"

Judith flushed with the knowledge of what her mother meant. "Leave Stratford?" she asked, her voice trailing off. She glanced again at her father but his eyes seemed unable to leave the ground. The creases in his forehead and the sorrow around his mouth made him look as heartbroken as Judith felt. The one thing that Judith had held on to through these past few weeks, the one saving grace that had always made her feel just a little bit better, was that her father hadn't found out about what had happened. That at least she hadn't disappointed him, her warm, kind, loving father. She'd been so grateful a moment such as this had never arrived, but now, it seemed, it had. This was the most unkindest cut of all.

"You can leave by week's end," Mary told her daughter, the abruptness of it startling Judith. She understood then that her mother believed that she was the cause of the evil spirits in the house and she was pushing her away; getting rid of her like she'd gotten rid of so many of Anne's things. Judith had a hard time taking in the rest of the travel details her mother went on describing. Judith's head thudded with the images of Master Hunt she'd suppressed these many weeks. She blinked and tried to shake them away. Judith looked again at her father, her knees shaking slightly, and tried to will him to look at her. She thought that if only he would smile at her, or comfort her like he used to do when she was a child, then everything might still be alright. Then maybe even this could be forgiven. But as her mother talked on her father never looked up, and in that moment it dawned on Judith that things had changed irrevocably.

6

Within a fortnight Judith had been shipped off to London. She arrived late on an autumn afternoon, her travelling party having ridden hard to get there before nightfall on the third day. As they approached the city from the north Judith initially mistook Shoreditch and its scattering of wooden buildings and tall lazy windmills as London itself, and was disappointed at the smallness of it. She'd heard so many spectacular things about the great city of London that she couldn't believe it could be that simple. But then she turned her head and saw open before her, like a multicolored butterfly spreading its wings, the marvelous panorama of London.

First were the red tiled roofs that went on for miles, piled in rows like carefully packed apples in a box for market. Here and there smoke filtered lazily from brick chimneys as the late afternoon sun glinted off weathervanes and windows of stained glass. Next Judith took in the architectural grandeur of Westminster Hall and the Abbey. Judith had set so many of her plays in London that she'd often wondered if her imaginings of the tall, spiky building were true to life; glimpsing it from a distance Judith realized that she'd only underestimated its cool, imposing beauty. To the east the Gothic gable and spire of St. Paul's Cathedral took Judith's breath away and she wondered how it was possible for man to create such large, beautiful buildings. And then Judith spied the solid, imposing turrets of the Tower of London and they spoke to her with the imaginings of all the people locked inside. Judith felt as if she could actually hear the tired, lonely sigh of the traitor, hungry and cold and longing for companionship as she clung to the bars of a small window in the bare, imposing structure. Judith shivered, despite the warm cloak wrapped around her shoulders.

Judith tore her eyes away from the city and looked at the road before her. They were heading into the heart of Shoreditch and Judith was taken aback by the pitifulness of the place up close. It was loud with the shouts and taunts of shopkeepers and their customers and dirty with refuse thrown in the streets. Swarms of unwashed street urchins followed their party, begging for coin and a little food. Judith was distracted from their tiny faces and heart-rending pleas only by the fight that broke out in front of a row of alehouses off to her left. A crowd of young men were gathering and cheering on the pugilists, whose red faces were puffy with drink and hubris. Judith looked about for someone to come and break up the fight, but much of the rest of the town seemed oblivious to the action, going about their business as if such things were an everyday occurrence. Judith held her breath and crossed her fingers and didn't relax until they were at Bishopsgate, the tall stone entrance to the city of London proper.

The portcullis was up when they arrived and the guardsmen on either side of the gate let the party through with barely a nod. Once on the other side of the old stone barrier and into the city itself Judith marveled at the transformation that took place. The streets were wider and cleaner, the buildings taller and statelier, and the inns and lodging houses that lined the main road were not nearly so dilapidated or rowdy. Even the stench from the city ditch seemed to recede on this side of the wall.

Her party stopped at the Angel, one of the larger inns for long-distance travelers, and many of the people she'd been traveling with quickly took rooms and disappeared inside the grey wooden building. Judith waited outside by the entrance, looking at the myriad of people that passed by on the street, waiting for a servant from the Mountjoys' to come and fetch her. Judith recognized no one, of course, and wondered what it would be like to live in a city where no one knew you, no one knew your past, no one could recite for you the history of your family. It seemed impossibly liberating.

As Judith waited many different kinds of people passed her on the street, some with dark complexions, some light, some dressed in rich threads of purple velvet, most in dirty homespun, young men with long, confident strides, old workers with short, mincing gaits. Judith was so struck by the variety of the place, by the new things and new people she was seeing, that she failed to notice a heavy, lumbering wagon that took up the entire width of the street as it came up upon her. It would have run her over, had a stranger not at the last moment pulled her inside the entranceway of the inn. Flushed and embarrassed she thanked the unknown man, but he merely nodded and disappeared into the establishment. Looking back down the street at the receding cart Judith was shocked by the driver's lack of care for anyone or anything in his path. For a moment she was angry, but then she smiled softly to herself. All this commotion and aloofness was alien to her, but she could tell already that it was a way of life she could get used to. The craziness of the city, somehow, allowed a measure of inner calm and serenity. When she'd left Stratford for London her mother's parting words to her were, *Be grateful to God. For everything.* In London, Judith nearly could.

After another hour of waiting, just as Judith began to think about counting her money and seeing if she could afford a bed for the night, a thin, broad-faced, dark colored girl approached the inn. She couldn't have been more than thirteen, maybe fourteen years old.

"Miss Shakespeare?"

Judith nodded.

"They call me Joan," the girl said, a wide smile spreading across her face. Her eyes twinkled in her dark complexion and

Judith thought that she had never seen anyone so beautiful before. "Follow me. I'll take you to where you're supposed to be."

Judith tried to keep up as Joan skipped down the busy street, turning suddenly down alleyways and side roads that left Judith hopelessly disoriented. She would have liked to have gone slower, and spent more time gazing at the buildings and people and wares that were for sale, but she was nervous about losing sight of Joan, who didn't seem much concerned at all with whether or not Judith was behind her.

After a few more turns they stopped before a tall, three-storey house in the northwest corner of the city. It had two gables and jettied upper floors and seemed impressively imposing.

"'Tis it," Joan said, standing with one hand on her hip and the other out before her. "Here, let me take that." She reached for the roll of clothes that Judith had been carrying since Stratford.

"How did you know it was me?" Judith asked, releasing the goods.

"Hm?"

"In front of the inn. How did you know I was the one you were looking for?"

Joan laughed. "You had that struck look on your face new people in London always have. As if they've just been hit with a board."

Judith smiled, a little embarrassed, and followed Joan into the back of the house.

Even at this late hour the place was alive with activity. Dough was being slapped in the kitchen, silver polished in the dining room, floors swept in the parlour. "There aren't any customers right now," Joan said, leading Judith to the front of the house, "so I can show you around." They entered a large, tastefully decorated foyer furnished with a sideboard, two wide chairs, and a porcelain vase full of flowers. There was even a gilded mirror on the wall which Judith instinctively shied away from, but Joan had no problem preening herself before.

"The first floor is mostly for the customers," Joan told Judith. "They come in and are entertained by a servant who serves them cake and something to drink. Then they're fitted in the rooms at the back of the house, and all that over there," Joan said, indicating the entire left wing of the house, "is where the apprentices actually make the headdresses. Mr. Mountjoy doesn't do much of the work anymore, he spends more of his time travelling about England trying to get the wives of dukes, earls, counts and barons to all come here for their tires. At least," Joan said conspiratorially, leaning in to where Judith stood, "that's what he gives as the reason for always leaving town."

"What other reason could he have?" Judith asked innocently, and Joan snickered like the little girl that she was.

They went up a flight of stairs. "Mr. and Mrs. Mountjoy sleep on this floor. Their rooms are over there," Joan waved toward the hall to the right of the stairwell. "And the little 'uns sleep over here on this side. Servants sleep on the top floor. You and I will be sharing a room, but we're lucky, it's only just us. Some of the other rooms have three or more apprentices in them at a time, especially when they need to open up a room for a guest."

Joan continued up the next flight of stairs and Judith followed her to the end of the hall. A bare wooden door creaked on its hinges and Judith felt a shiver of nervousness as it opened on her new surroundings. She was reminded of the door at the Palace of the Sun in Ovid's *Metamorphoses*, the intricately carved door that opened on an entirely new world.

Inside the room were two small plain beds, a desk and chair, a dry sink, and an armoire. A casement window let in the afternoon's fading light. Judith walked over to it and pressed her hand against the cool panes of glass. "I bet you get good sun in the mornings," she said, looking down into the street.

"Too much," Joan confirmed. "That's why I sleep on the bed closest to the wall. You can have this one." She put Judith's clothes on the end of the bed nearest the window.

"Thank you," Judith replied, still looking out the window. After a moment she turned and asked, "Have you been here all your life? In London, I mean?"

Joan nodded slightly. "For as long as I can remember."

Judith cocked her head and pursed her lips, considering the indirectness of the answer. Joan was surprised as most people didn't listen closely enough to realize that the answer was in fact a hedge.

"Do you have kin here? In London?" Joan didn't reply so Judith continued. "I've never seen a blackamoor before."

The familiar annoyance when anyone brought up her foreign skin or hair or background flared in Joan. She liked to pretend that she was indeed born in London, sometimes even to the Mountjoy family. But her annoyance faded quickly. Judith was so earnest in her curiosity, so innocent in her questions that it was hard to stay offended. Joan surprised herself by answering her new roommate honestly.

"I was freed from a captured Spanish ship," she paused, studying Judith's reaction. "When I was a baby." She turned then and went to the door. "We better introduce you to the mistress before she starts wondering what I've done with you."

When they walked into the sitting room on the second floor they found Mrs. Mountjoy resting in an embroidered armchair, her skirts spread out in folds before her, a small leather book open in her hands. Judith was afraid of interrupting her quietude, but Joan didn't show any hesitation. She crossed the threshold into the room and Mrs. Mountjoy looked up, her sky blue eyes sharp as ice. "There you are!"

Judith entered the room but stopped a few feet from her mistress and curtsied shakily.

"Come here so I can have a look at you."

Judith walked closer. Mrs. Mountjoy was beautiful, that was for sure. She had high, rounded cheekbones, a smooth, broad forehead, and the most perfectly clear skin Judith had ever seen. She didn't need makeup or covering wax at all. She wore her thick brown hair in a pile on top of her head and the mass of it emphasized her delicate, regal neck.

"They didn't tell me you were so beautiful," Mrs. Mountjoy said to Judith, surprising her with the echo of her own thoughts. Judith spied a table in the corner of the room, piled high with leather-bound volumes like the one in Mrs. Mountjoy's hands.

"You arrived late," Mrs. Mountjoy said. "Have you had supper yet?"

But Judith was having a hard time keeping her gaze from the books in the corner. She'd never seen so many volumes before, all in one place. She'd had no idea so many books had even been written. Were they all by the same person, she wondered?

"What are you looking at?" her mistress asked, turning to see what had captured Judith's attention. "Those books in the corner?"

Judith tore her eyes away. "'Tis an honor to meet you, Mistress Mountjoy." She smiled and curtsied shakily again.

Mrs. Mountjoy looked at her new maidservant curiously. Without a word she held up the volume in her hands and, after an exchanged glance, Judith took it. She turned it over carefully, running her fingers along its ridged, delicate spine.

"Can you read?" Mrs. Mountjoy asked.

Judith paused, her hands starting to sweat uncomfortably.

"I'd appreciate having a maidservant that could read to me when my eyes got tired," Mrs. Mountjoy encouraged.

Judith was unsure what to say. Her mother, she knew, would tell her to deny such an unmaidenly skill, but she got the sense that Mrs. Mountjoy didn't seem to consider reading a bad trait. Judith hesitated, tension gathering in the spaces of the silence around them, until she finally decided that the temptation was just too great; the possibility of reading all those books was positively mouth watering. "I can."

"Wonderful!" Mrs. Mountjoy exclaimed. "I had no idea I was getting such an educated maidservant."

Relief spread through Judith's shoulders and the smile that crept across her face was genuine this time.

"Thank you for bringing her here," Mrs. Mountjoy said, turning to Joan, who took the hint and left the room.

"You're going to have to tell me how it is you learned to read, my dear. You're lucky, you know, most women aren't given the chance."

Judith nodded, still a bit in awe of her beautiful mistress.

"But for now just sit by my side, here, and tell me about your journey from Stratford. I don't believe I've ever been to Stratford. There's a little river that runs through it, is there not?"

Judith took a seat on the footstool by her mistress' side and carefully answered all of her questions. Mrs. Mountjoy seemed sincerely interested, and even when she leaned back and closed her eyes, Judith could tell she was still listening. Judith fell in love with her worldly mistress that day, and over the next few years her affection and loyalty for her only grew.

Mrs. Mountjoy as well took a liking to Judith, showing her around town and answering even her most curious of questions. They spent many afternoons together reading books and discussing some of the ideas in them, Mrs. Mountjoy making sure that Judith knew Latin and even a little Greek. There were still boundaries to their relationship, which Judith painfully discovered when she questioned, once, the amount of time her mistress spent with the Earl of Bath. Mrs. Mountjoy pointedly reminded Judith that a woman could be as chaste as ice and as pure as snow and still not escape calumny. Then she'd told Judith never to question her again, and Judith never did. She liked her new life in London too much.

She liked waking up every morning and helping her mistress dress and pick out jewelry for the day, she liked walking about the busy streets of London, she liked smelling foreign perfumes and eating unfamiliar foods, and mostly, she just liked feeling that she belonged. Judith warmed to the order and routine of her days with the Mountjoys; she felt safe, comfortable, and useful in her new life. There were times, late at night, when she couldn't sleep and her mind wandered to thoughts of her brothers and sisters, especially poor little Anne up in heaven. Sometimes she crawled out of bed, snuck into the workroom on the first floor, and gazed at all the silver and gold thread on the workbench, the glittering jewels in their tiny containers, and imagined all the costumes and props she could make with the sumptuous materials.

But Judith was a woman now, and for the most part she'd put away her silly fantasies of plays and stage acting. She was living in a respectable house, with a respectable family, and she spent every day trying to live up to the responsibility. She worked hard, kept herself modest, and when Mrs. Mountjoy didn't need her of an afternoon because she was out of town or lunching with a friend, Judith didn't fritter away the time at a pub or a bearbating like Joan and the other servants inevitably did, she found something useful to do. One afternoon she was sitting in her room translating Latin when she was interrupted by the creak of the door.

"Judith? Are you in here?" It was Joan, her wide eyes peering around the door frame.

"Yay."

"What are you doing? Not reading again," Joan said, a note of exhaustion in her voice. She slipped into the room and flitted about, pulling the coverlet on her bed, straightening the towel by the dry sink, in general trying to get Judith's attention. "Doesn't it hurt your eyes?" Joan didn't wait for an answer but twirled in a circle and landed with a thump on Judith's bed. "We have an entire afternoon of freedom. What say we go to a bearbaiting?"

Judith never could understand Joan's penchant for bloody entertainment. Every time another prisoner from the Tower of London was set to be hanged, Joan made every effort to be at the spectacle. When walking across the London Bridge Joan always glanced at the rotting heads pierced on stakes at the southern end. And whenever she had a chance to see a couple of wild dogs tear at a bear unfairly roped to a post, she went. It wasn't Judith's thing, but Joan sure enjoyed it.

"Nay, I'll stay here."

"You can't sit in this tiny room all day," Joan said in something of a whine.

"I shan't," Judith replied. "I'll go to the Mitre for supper later."

Joan considered her arguments. "You only go to that boring alehouse because they give out free candles with supper and you can sit and read all night."

Judith closed the book before her and sighed. "So?"

"You have to have fun sometime!"

"But I am having fun. Reading is fun. You should try it some time," Judith said, and then felt guilty for reminding Joan of her inability to read. Judith sighed, wishing mostly to be left alone. She turned towards Joan. "Ok, ok, I'll go. Just let me get dressed."

Joan picked up the book that Judith had set aside and idly flipped through its pages, pretending to take an interest in the printed words. "You know," she suggested, "we could go to a show at the newly opened Theatre in Shoreditch. Would you prefer that instead? I've heard good things about it, including that it gets so crowded in the front pit you can't go a single act without a pinch on the bum!"

Judith laughed as she struggled to pin up her hair. "How far outside of town is it?"

"About a mile. 'Tis a nice day," Joan added, going to the window. "It wouldn't be a bad walk."

"How much does it cost?" Judith asked, worried that she didn't have enough money for a show and for supper later.

"A penny. Just like bearbaiting."

Judith couldn't explain why the thought of going to the Theatre made her nervous, but it did. Ever since it had opened the year before she'd wanted to go, she had truly wanted to see the plays and the actors and the costumes, but she'd hesitated out of some unexplained nervousness. Too many memories of her childhood and play-acting back home? Fear that it would never compare to the traveling players that used to come to Stratford? Worry that if she went just once, she'd find excuses to keep going back until she'd spent all her money and gotten in trouble? Judith hesitated, knowing that there would probably be no going back once she stepped over the initial precipice.

"Ok," she finally agreed, slipping on her shoes. Nerves be damned. "Let's try the Theatre."

The performance that day was a comedy, a skit about a pair of young brothers in love with the same woman. As it turned out, their one woman was actually two (twins), so that in the end each man had his woman and everyone was happy. Judith was lost in the play five minutes after it began. Easily she let herself be transported to the imaginary town in Italy where the story took place. When the brothers first saw their lady loves, walking in a field out across a stream, without effort Judith's heart mirrored their own. She felt their angst and was tormented by their desire. As the women began to show interest in the brothers, Judith's own adrenaline quickened. When, at last, they all came together before the priest to be married Judith couldn't help herself, she jumped up and down and clapped her hands. She wasn't the only one; many other audience members were bouncing on their feet and yelling congratulations towards the stage, but Judith could easily have been the audience member most invested. The degree to which her heart opened up and drank in every word of the performance surprised even Judith. It was as if her soul had been asleep these many, long years, and suddenly it was pushed, blinking, into the light.

The props for the performance had been few, but the stage itself was a wonder to behold. It was huge, and exactly the right height for everyone to see. It had numerous entrances and exits so that the transitions of the actors were smooth and uncontrived. Parts of the middle section of the stage turned out to be false, dropping down and out of sight when necessary for an actor to suddenly disappear. After most of the audience had left Judith still stood in the middle of the pit, gazing at the stage, wondering who had built such a marvelous structure and how all its mysteries worked.

"Anon, let's go," Joan said, tugging at Judith's sleeve.

"You go. I want to stay a few minutes longer."

Joan knew that Judith was a little curious, but why she would want to stand around in an empty pit when the action was over Joan couldn't understand. She decided not to press the matter. Let Judith do what she wanted, the night was young and there was still time to have more fun before the mistress returned. Joan was determined to enjoy herself and not stand aimlessly about in an abandoned playhouse, so she left and didn't give another thought to how Judith was going to make her own way home.

Standing there, Judith realized just how strongly she missed her younger siblings, and how much she yearned to playact with them again in the forest. It'd been years since she'd sat around inventing skits in her head, but the love of story-making that she'd tried to bury these last few years, in an attempt to grow up and become a responsible woman, had clearly never been deeply interred. With a wave of nostalgia that nearly made her weep, Judith knew that she'd come home. That this was exactly where she was supposed to be.

"Can I help you?"

Judith looked around, startled. Standing in the yard, off to the right, was an elderly gentleman in breeches and fashionable doublet. He looked to be about her father's age, and he had kind eyes like her father too. His hair was short and neatly trimmed and he sported a spade beard, the kind more often seen on soldiers and younger men.

"I- I-" Judith cleared her throat. "I was just standing here."

"I can see that. The play's over, you know. There won't be another one til tomorrow." James wondered for a moment if this was another crazy. One of those people who thought the play itself was real and wanted to go home with the actors back to Italy, or the forest, or wherever the current story was set. She was a little young to be one of the harlots that offered themselves to the actors after the performances, he thought, but you never knew.

"Who are you?"

"Who am I?" James was impressed with the boldness of the question. "I'm James Burbage. Owner and manager of this playhouse, and I'm trying to clear the pit so I can shut down for the night."

Immediately Judith was embarrassed. The owner and manager of this amazing place. She didn't know what to say. She had so many questions she wanted to ask. Without being able to control it, one popped out. "What's under the stage, underneath the trap doors?"

James walked towards Judith. "Now that is a question I don't normally get asked. That's one of my innovations," he told her proudly. "I call it the cellar - the actors call it the dungeon - because it's just an open space below the stage for the players to wait for their cues. There's no light, except what filters through from tiny pinholes in the stage floor, so I guess it can seem somewhat scary under there, a little like a dungeon." He smiled. "I built it because I thought it'd be good for ghost scenes, to have ghosts be able to rise from the floor. We've ended up using it for so much more, including fight scenes to get rid of the bodies, quick escape scenes during comedies, and as a way to get certain props on and off the stage."

"Your casting of Viola wasn't quite right."

James raised his eyebrows, surprised again by this odd young woman with the clear blue eyes.

"Women aren't *that* stupid. They know when a man is following them."

"Do they now?"

"James!" A strong male voice yelled out from the tiring house behind the stage.

"Here man!"

A small, stocky fellow emerged. "Oh, there you are. We're off to the Bull."

"I'm coming." James turned to Judith with a gleam in his eye. "Would you like to join us for a drink? You can tell Viola herself why her portrayal was incomplete."

Judith blushed red, but then nodded her assent.

They made a large crowd, James, Judith, John Perkin and John Laneham - the two actors who played the pair of brothers; William Johnson and Thomas Clarke - the actors who played the twin sisters; Robert Wilson - the buffoon who turned the part of the mother of the sisters into a blundering fool. He also played the part of the prankster, Mole, who followed the brothers around the stage making narrative, somewhat offensive asides to the audience. There were also a few men seated at the table not directly a part of the troupe: Richard Tarlton was an actor in a different company who, like Robert Wilson, specialized in clownish roles, and John Lyly and Robert Greene were both local playwrights.

"It's not often you invite your women to the pub with us beforehand," John Lyly ribbed James.

"I haven't taken her home with me, yet," James winked playfully at Judith. "Nay, she's here to inform Will how to play a woman better, aren't you, Miss Judith?"

"What, didn't I walk right? Not enough hip in my stride?" Will got up and pranced around the table, jutting his hips in an exaggerated fashion from side to side, to the loud cheers and claps of the other patrons in the pub.

"Nay, nay, 'tis like this." Richard got up this time and walked around the table with his hands fanned out in front of his face, peering slightly now and again from behind them as he pretended to be coy and somewhat afraid of all the big, strong men. John Lyly pinched him on the arse as he passed and Richard didn't miss a beat, jumping into the air and squealing with fake embarrassment. The table roared with laughter.

"Are you new to London?" Robert Greene asked Judith kindly.

"Not that new. I've been here a few years. As servant to Mistress Mountjoy."

The name brought muffled guffaws to the table and Judith looked around in confusion.

"Mrs. Mountjoy," John Laneham said, slapping John Perkin on the back. "John certainly knows her."

"I suppose you could say I'm familiar with her." John Perkin agreed.

The other men at the table watched Judith to see how she would respond, to see if she got the veiled reference to the affair John and Mary had carried on the year before. Judith was not unaware of her mistresses indiscretions so she replied, "She got tired of you too after awhile, eh?"

The table burst out in laughter. James squeezed Judith's hand and she knew she had said the right thing, that now she was accepted.

They spent many hours at the pub together that night, drinking and telling stories. Judith learned that John Laneham had been an actor since he was just ten years old, originally travelling the countryside in smaller troupes of boy players. He'd been to Newcastle, Manchester, Liverpool, and what seemed to Judith as almost the whole of England. He'd played the roles of kings, queens, fools, ghosts, gods, and even an animal or two. In an earlier year he'd been caught by the Queen's Men in violation of the vagabond law. Without much prompting he lifted his shirt and showed Judith the brand burned into his skin for the crime.

Robert Greene was either a lady's man, or just had the good fortune of befriending many famous women. Judith couldn't tell if it were really true or not, but the table claimed that he was a confidant of the wealthy Bess Hardwick, Countess of Shrewsbury, that he'd had a love affair with the learned (and much older) Elizabeth Cooke, Lady Hoby, and that he once dined with Levina Teerlinc, the court painter to Queen Elizabeth. Later Judith came to believe that at least some of it must be true because Robert was the only man she knew who truly seemed to understand women - he always listened to their questions and treated them with respect, and he never sounded surprised or defensive when a woman's argument was proved right over a man's opinion. He had a bright, pointy red beard that on that first night Judith noticed was well groomed and without an ounce of food in it.

Thomas Clarke, originally from Rowington near Judith's hometown, had come to London as a carpenter's apprentice, but to the profound disappointment of his family left after a few years to join the Theatre. He'd been unable to help it, he told Judith - who fully understood - but now he owed the family he formerly apprenticed for a substantial sum of money for his earlier years of room and board. Even worse, his father had never forgiven him. "And he probably never will," Thomas told Judith. "He's a Puritan." Judith was informed by the other men at the table that Thomas' father had only grown more extreme over the years since his son had joined the troupe, and that he now regularly preached diatribes in the streets against the evils of playacting. The elder Clarke believed that playacting was a form of devil worship, because only an evil spirit would give his son the delusional impulse to act the part of gods. Thomas' father had never actually seen a play, or gone to one of his son's performances, but that didn't diminish his certitude.

Judith was surprised that through most of the evening Robert Wilson remained quiet. He'd played such loud, clownish roles in the play earlier that evening that to see him so calm at the pub seemed out of character. Or maybe this was the real Robert and the Robert on stage was the one out of character? Judith didn't know, but she wondered. At a break in the conversation she asked him why he seemed so reserved, while on stage he'd been so wild, and he replied, "but that is the beauty of acting, my dear, you can be someone else for awhile. You need not be you."

Judith found this profound.

"Fie, fie, 'tisn't it," James told her. "The truth is he's an actor, and a playwright too. He's busy observing us and taking mental notes for his next script. Beware, you just may be in it now."

Judith looked at Robert in fright, but he only smiled, neither confirming nor denying anything anybody would say about him. He remained a mystery over the next few months as Judith returned to both the playhouse and the pub afterwards, night after night, just as she'd feared, spending all her time and all her money in the company of the Leicester's Men.

7

Morning dawned on another cold day. The rain on the windowsill crystallized into icicles as Judith stared and waited for inspiration. She pulled the thin wool blanket tighter around her shoulders and sighed. As a child she'd had so many ideas for stories and plays, but now she couldn't seem to think of any. Judith had been certain, after spending so many months at the Theatre and talking so often with John Lyly and Robert Greene, that if she just spent a few focused hours on it, she'd be able to write something good. But now that her mistress was away for the day and Judith had some uninterrupted time to herself, she could come up with nothing.

Fidgeting in the wooden chair that faced the small desk, Judith picked up the paper she'd saved for months to buy and brought it close to her face. She pressed her nose up against its crinkly pale sheets and inhaled, imagining words in dark curly script printed on the clean open page. The paper smelled faintly of wet dog and, she thought, tree birch.

She remembered Robert Greene, after three beers and a mincemeat pie, emphasizing how a play should never be too realistic, too moralistic, or too learned. That was the job of the preachers, he told her. People came to plays to laugh, to forget their own lives for a couple of hours, to be entertained. Above all else, entertainment was the goal. Judith tried to keep that in mind as she went through story lines in her head.

She considered writing about a king lost at sea, stranded after a terrible storm on a deserted island, spending his time learning how to hunt and build, just like any common man, until eventually he learns to divine the gods through sorcery... Furiously Judith began writing, pouring out an opening scene of shipwreck, destitution, and hopelessness. After two pieces of precious paper had been covered by tiny black scrawl, Judith stopped. She reread the pages. They were horrible. She could hear everyone at the pub telling her that to portray a king as a common man was not funny whatsoever. She wondered if it'd be better if the king were a duke? But no, the plot was just too serious. It wasn't amusing at all.

Judith picked up the ruined pieces of paper and started to tear them in two lengthwise, but then stopped. It seemed a crime to throw away precious paper, even if the writing on it wasn't any good. She had no idea what else she could do with the used paper, but ripping it apart seemed somehow wrong. Carefully Judith smoothed the sheets and put them into a pile before starting anew.

A story that begins with a ghost? Judith had always loved plays that involved apparitions, sorcery, or witchcraft. Until she was thirteen years old she'd left bowls of cream out at night for the fairies to drink, even though her mother had reprimanded her for being wasteful. While she knew the church taught that ghosts were devils in disguise, Judith liked to believe they were more benign than that. That when they came to earth they came with a purpose, and often that purpose was to help others.

Judith opened her play with the ghost of a loving father who appeared one night in order to help his son. He wanted to tell his son to follow his dream, to stay a student and become a scholar, and not return home to the land where his uncle now ruled as a despotic overlord. It was a serious opening, shocking even with the ghost and apparition, but Judith could argue that it would at least catch the audience's attention. Drawing out the characters of the son, the father, and the uncle with names and descriptions, Judith began to think that the story had real appeal. She wrote a long monologue where the son debated with himself the veracity of the apparition that was his father. She stalled, though, when it came time to explain the reason for the uncle's overbearance. What drives a man to treat his own nephew as if he were a slave? Ambition? Heartache? Judith considered a number of factors, but eventually gave up. Her story was getting away again from the amusing tone Robert insisted all good plays required. With a sigh, Judith added these sheets to the disregarded pile. She looked out the window and gazed at the spire of St. Paul's in the distance.

Judith had been avoiding it because it seemed so childish and womanly, but her mind was drawn to a play about a princess. A beautiful princess whom everyone in the land wished to marry. The king, knowing his daughter is heavily sought after, invents a series of riddles that any potential suitor must solve before gaining the chance to even court the princess. Strong, handsome, wealthy men from across the kingdom come and attempt the riddles, but one after the other they fail miserably. The problem, the King's court jester realizes one day after watching the scene play out time and again, is that the suitors all believe the riddles complex, with learned and difficult answers. It dawns on the jester that in fact the riddles are designed to display the sincerity and simplicity of an honest, good man. Knowing this, the jester dresses up in disguise and attempts the riddles himself. The King is overjoyed when they are finally solved and, when the jester's true identity is revealed, the audience learns that the princess was in love with him all along. The play ends with a large, joyous, magnificent royal wedding.

It wasn't bad, Judith considered, reading over the pages. But something wasn't exactly right either. She stood up out of the hard, straight-backed chair, dropped the blanket that had been itching her neck, and stretched her arms overhead. Looking out the window Judith noticed with surprise that the sun had made its way high in the sky, and that the morning was nearly half over. She needed to find some chore to busy herself with so it wouldn't look like she'd been idle. Putting all the paper under her bed and neatly tucking the ink and quill in a corner of the windowsill, Judith opened the door, only to find Joan waiting there in something of a crouch.

"I- I was trying not to disturb you, because you hate it when I disturb you, but, well, here," Joan stood up and thrust a neatly folded epistle in Judith's direction, "this just came for you."

Judith turned the letter over and looked at the signet imprinted in red sealing wax. It looked to be from her family, back in Stratford. She wondered with a mixture of excitement and fear what they could possibly by writing her about. She sat down on the edge of the bed, Joan getting comfortable beside her, and cracked the sealing wax.

Dear Sister,

It has been such a long time since we've seen each other. I trust you are doing well, and that London is to your liking. Henry, the vintner's son from down the street - do you remember him? The one who used to keep rabbits as pets and always fell asleep two rows ahead of us in church, snoring with his head tilted impossibly to the side - he returned recently to Stratford from a trip to London and told us that he ran into you at the Maiden Head in Cripplegate. It was a like a long draught quenching a parching thirst, to finally hear about my sweet sister Judith again. You've been gone so long now, I can barely remember, is your hair still the color of summer wheat? Are you still tall and thin, or has your back broken from all the hard work and toil? What IS the notorious Mrs. Mountjoy like?

As for myself, I've gotten into a mountain of trouble lately for skipping school and taking long walks north past the cornfields towards Shottery. On a warm and beautiful day, when the birds are singing and the flowers are delicately opening their buds, who can help it? The truth is, I'm thinking about quitting school anyway. I know 'tis early, but what else can Master Hunt teach me? He turned rather abrasive after you left, and reciting Latin is just not as much fun as it used to be. Plus, a scrivener's apprenticeship opened up with John Fisher down Henley Street. I could make a lot of money one day as a lawyer, and, well, we need it.

To be perfectly honest, dear Judith, I am writing to inform you of our family's current troubles. 'Tis nothing to worry about, or try to rush home for, but father has been noted among a list of recusants for failing to attend Church services. And you know father, rather than pay the fine and take the oath of allegiance to our Protestant queen, he has simply stopped attending council meetings altogether. The Badgers, Reynolds, and Nashes are all in the same situation with us, which is helping our friends on the council provide a more unified front in protecting everyone, but it does not look good. Meanwhile, the brogue James Langrake cheated father on yet another wool deal, I know not by exactly how much, but it must be near four hundred pounds. Crops are not growing well in Snitterfield this year. Everyone is hurting.

Rereading that last paragraph it all sounds so gloomy. Things are not as bad as all that - baby Edmund, who was born just after you left, is healthy as a colt and the rest of us, god bless us, have our health too. Father has also arranged a few land deals among the cousins to raise some money. I just wanted you to know that your bright, beautiful presence is missed around here, especially these days. If you get the chance, it would do a spot of good if you surprised us with a word. Everyone would love to hear from you, including mother.

Your loving brother,
William

Judith clutched the letter to her chest. She couldn't tell if the emotion she was feeling was worry about her family, joy that little William had written her, or wonder that her mother might finally have forgiven her. Already she was composing a reply in her head. Joan, still sitting on the edge of the bed next to Judith, leaned in closer and asked, "Well?"

"'Tis from my brother, William."

"And?"

"And he sends news about the family."

Joan waited but Judith offered nothing else. She was thinking about her family's troubles, and the risk William had taken writing her about it.

"'Tis pretty handwriting," Joan commented.

Judith looked down at the letter and thought, yes, I suppose William does have a nice script.

"It means he's creative. And strong."

"And strong?" Judith turned finally to look at Joan. "You have some of the silliest notions. How do you get strong out of this letter?"

"Look at that swoop there," Joan said, pointing. "How long it is. It means he's strong. Or, that he has long fingers."

Judith laughed out loud, wondering what William would make of Joan if he ever met her. Would he imagine her in all sorts of plays and as a range of possible characters, as Judith herself often did? "Let's go downstairs," Judith said, "and find some work to do before the mistress comes home and we get into trouble."

At the pub that night Judith was eager to tell her friends about the play she'd begun with the princess, jester, and riddles. When she arrived, however, cold from the early winter air, only Robert Greene and John Lyly were seated at the troupe's usual table near the back of the hall. Judith joined them as they ate supper.

"Sunflower," Robert said, greeting Judith with his preferred nickname.

Judith winced. At least he hadn't called her bumblebee, she thought, or corn stalk, which was even worse because it referred to both her yellow hair and her unmaidenly height. She really didn't like all the nicknames she'd somehow acquired.

"I've been writing all afternoon," she told them, getting comfortable on the bench opposite Robert.

John grunted while continuing to delve into his food.

"The play I like best takes place at court. It-"

"Court? Whose court?" Robert interrupted.

"I- Well- I hadn't thought about that yet. Does it matter?"

"Of course it matters. The audience needs to know where and when things take place. The actors need to know how to prepare."

"Ok. I hadn't decided on it yet, but ok. It takes place in Italy, last century."

Robert nodded and let Judith continue.

"'Tis about a king and his beautiful daughter whose looks are famous across the land. The king knows many suitors will travel to seek her hand, so he needs to find a way to choose a good man among the many despoilers that will arrive."

John pushed his cleared trencher away and stifled a yawn.

"Eventually," Judith added, watching John out of the corner of her eye, "the king decides on a series of riddles that only a good and honest man can solve."

Robert, who'd been distracted by a group of rowdy men at a table off to his right, returned his attention to Judith. "Sounds good so far," he said, leaning back and stroking his red pointy beard, "but as a story, not as a play."

Judith hadn't finished, but she stopped to listen to Robert.

"The audience needs something to watch; you need to keep the action going at all times. Having a bunch of actors standing about discussing riddles won't work, there needs to be something for the audience to see."

"'Tis true," John agreed, picking his teeth.

At first Judith didn't know what to say. She hadn't finished describing the idea, let alone gotten around to discussing the stage action or the props for the scenes. It felt premature, but Robert was a successful and famous playwright; his opinions mattered and his thoughts were worth listening to.

A beer maiden came by then to collect payment for the men's supper and Judith watched as she took Robert and John's coins over to the manager behind the counter. He was a large, imposing figure and as he pulled a rectangular box out from behind the counter to make change for the girl, his eye caught Judith's and he winked.

"The riddles are posted on a series of boxes," Judith suddenly decided. "A gold box, a silver box, and a lead box."

Robert nodded, but John guffawed. "Lead? Who wants a lead box? Make the last one pewter, so they're all worth something."

"Nay, but that's the point," Judith realized, discovering the solution to her own riddle as she spoke. "Lead is indeed something nobody wants, especially when compared to silver or gold. But 'tis the lead box that holds the answer to the King's riddle. Only a man who doesn't care for money, who can see beyond outward glittery appearances and apparent wealth, will choose the lead box, and that's the one the king wants for his daughter. The suitor who realizes all that glitters is not gold, the suitor who wants her, and not the king's fortune, is the one worth marrying."

Robert admitted to himself that it was good, especially for a woman. John, however, snickered scornfully. From the beginning John had been critical of Judith's attempts to write a play, not believing that a woman had the wit or the humor for it. He'd made his skepticism plain in his inattention and off-putting comments over the last few weeks, but Judith had kept trying anyway. She'd kept coming in week after week with new plot ideas and different character suggestions. She hadn't realized that John was simply waiting for the day she got tired of it.

A commotion at the entrance to the pub interrupted their conversation. The Leicester's Men had arrived and were trying to make their way inside. John Perkin and William Johnson were stuck in the doorway, as they insisted on walking through together, their arms around each other's shoulders. They sang a bawdy tune, loud and off-key, and waved enthusiastically to Judith, John, and Robert at the back of the hall. John Laneham and Richard Tarlton straggled through the door next, also rather tipsy. Behind them was Thomas Clarke, face paint still visible on his ears and neck. Judith's heart warmed at the sight of them all. Only at the end of the group did Judith spy James, the man she most wanted to see. As manager of the Theatre he was the one she had to convince of the soundness of her plays, for he was the one who had the power to actually put them on. But when James walked into the pub Judith's heart sank; his face was grave and off-putting and it was clear that something was wrong. He seemed to be dragging Robert Wilson into the pub behind him, reluctantly and with difficulty.

William told them what happened as he sat down at the table.

"Wilson got drunk again before the performance," he said, motioning to the beer maiden for a fresh tankard. "You should've seen it. He was so rich he stumbled across the stage, mixing up his lines and tripping over his feet. 'Twas pretty funny," he admitted, stifling a grin as he glanced in James' direction. "But in the fourth act, where he carries the torch, you know, Wilson dropped it and nearly caught the stage on fire. James," William said, shaking his head severely, "was not pleased."

"'Tis it," they all heard James' gravelly voice state as he approached the table with Wilson. "We can not do this. We'd be finished if the Theatre burnt down. Ruined. D'ye hear, man? Ruined."

Wilson nodded but you could tell he was having a hard time paying attention. He looked around the room, desperate for another drink.

"Listen to me," James said, trying to get him to focus. "You're a good actor and a good friend. In sooth, I'd hate to lose you, but you have got to stop this. Not when there's a performance."

"Yeah, drink on your own time," Thomas unsuccessfully joked.

Robert's roving eye settled for a minute on Judith, quiet at the end of the table.

"D'ye hear me, man?" James asked again.

Robert's eyes narrowed and his look turned cruel as he continued to stare at Judith. She turned away, wishing to avoid the tormented, unhappy eyes of Robert Wilson.

"Another round of drinks," John Lyly shouted. "The show's over, might as well keep his spirits up now."

James sighed and sat down heavily on the bench. John Lyly asked about how the rest of the performance had gone and the discussion evolved into a debate about whether the audience had really understood the innuendos in the second act or not. Judith looked for an opening to bring up her ideas to James; she wished she was sitting closer to him and not far away at the end of the table, but it didn't matter. Now was really not the time for such a discussion.

The drinks continued to arrive and disappear until Robert, thoroughly inebriated, could barely hold his head up. Most of the table had forgotten all about him until, like a dog who hears a sudden high-pitched whistle, he jerked himself straight and stared directly at Judith. Through grunts and groans he gathered his strength and pulled himself up out of his seat. Raising one arm he announced so all could hear, "She cheated on me! Cheated on me with a dolt! D'ye hear? With an unworthy churl!" Robert was swaying on his feet, yelling his ire to the entire pub, spittle gathering at the side of his mouth. James on his left and Richard Tarlton on his right tried to get him back in his seat, but Robert's anger was too powerful. He wrested an arm away and pointed it at Judith.

"Your kind should not be allowed out. You should be chained to a post like a dog, yes, like a dog. And when you're good we'll throw a bone at ye. Though everyone knows," Robert laughed in a gulping, rough fashion, "that'll never happen." Wresting both arms away from James and Richard, Robert leaned on the table for a minute, his head bowed for support. When he looked up the hate in his eyes had not abated. "What in hell is she doing here anyway?" Robert looked around the table for an answer. "'Tisn't right, her being here. She's not one of us."

For six months Judith had been hoping no one would notice that she didn't belong, that she wasn't really one of the troupe. She'd enjoyed their company so much, and was drawn to their performances so irresistibly, that she'd let herself believe it was ok to hang around with the Leicester's Men every evening, when the truth was, of course, that indeed she didn't belong. She stuck out in this circle of men like a rotten kernel in a cob of smooth yellow corn.

"Since when do we bring our whores with us to the pub beforehand?" Robert continued, his harangue getting ever louder.

Judith's face flamed red. She wondered why Robert was picking on her. She thought she had found a measure of companionship and understanding with the troupe, but Robert seemed to be taking that away from her. Why was she always being told that she had to live a certain way, act a certain way, be a certain kind of person? Deep down, underneath it all, underneath the breasts and the hair and the skin and the fingernails, wasn't she the same as them? If pricked, didn't she bleed? If poisoned, wouldn't she die? If yelled at, wasn't she shamed?

"You're not being fair," Judith said. Robert Greene reached under the table and tried to hold Judith's hand in a calming fashion, but she wasn't interested in his silent, invisible support.

"The devil speaks!"

"Don't be cross, Robert. What have I done?"

"Women are but an evil temptation! The bible tells us they were made for no other reason than to tempt us into evil!"

Judith knew that Robert wasn't making any sense and that she should just let it go, but for some reason, she couldn't. She had undue confidence in Robert's ability, and desire, to see through the fog. "Alas, I am your friend," Judith tried.

"My friend?" Robert spluttered. "You're not my friend. You're the problem. You and all the ones like you, with your pretty hair and your pretty skirts and your vanity, lies, insincerity, and temptation."

Judith felt the eyes of not just the table now, but much of the rest of the pub also staring down on her. Without warning something clicked in her breast. For too long she'd put up with nonsense such as this. For too long she'd kept quiet. When as a child she'd been told that girls weren't good for much, she'd simply agreed. When she'd been told she couldn't go to school because of her sex, she'd meekly submitted. When she'd been raped, she'd never even questioned the assumption that it had all been her fault. But not anymore. All those books she'd read from the Mountjoys' library had convinced her that things could be different. Aristotle said that independent observation was more important, and often more correct, than traditional authority.

Copernicus believed that the sun might actually be the center of the universe, not the earth. Montaigne even questioned the assumption that humans were superior amongst the animals! They all taught her that things could be different than conventionally believed. They all taught her to make up her own mind. Judith looked Robert in the eye. "The problem," she unwisely ventured, unable, suddenly, to control herself, "is that you failed to keep your woman happy."

Robert leapt across the table, his arms in the air, ready to strangle Judith. Before he could get to her Richard, James and John Lyly grabbed him by the arms and legs and pulled him back. Struggling, they dragged him to the front of the pub and out the door to cool off.

"It really wasn't his fault," Thomas leaned over and said to Judith. "She really did cheat on him."

But now there was no going back. The voice of her mistress seemed to have risen within Judith and come through as her own. "Yes, but why did she cheat on him?"

Thomas opened his mouth, and then shut it again. He looked at Judith quizzically, then shook his head. Judith could see the levers in his mind tripping over each other, running into confusion. Judith knew, in that moment, that if it ever came down to it, in an argument between herself and John Perkin, say, the most notorious womanizer in the group, he would be listened to and she wouldn't even be heard. It wasn't that these men, her friends, refused to see her side of things, it was that they simply weren't able.

"Are you upsetting the ladies again, Thomas?" A man Judith had never seen before came up behind them and rested a hand on Thomas' shoulder. "You must forgive my friend here, Miss-?"

"Judith."

"Miss Judith, with the lovely blue eyes. He's a theater man, and they never know what they are saying."

Judith was annoyed with the sudden interruption by this stranger, but when she turned and looked at the offender, her temper was replaced with shock. He was the most handsome man she had ever seen. He was tall, strong, well built, and the thick muscles of his forearms flexed firmly as he gripped Thomas' shoulder. His dark brown hair was long, and somewhat curly, and a single forelock fell into his eyes as he leaned towards them. His black eyes had an expression in them that Judith's heart seemed to recognize. She felt as if she'd seen this man before, but certainly if she had she would have remembered him. She didn't know if it was the argument she'd just had with Wilson, or the sudden presence of this attractive stranger, but her heart now beat uncomfortably within her chest.

"Cuthbert, my good man! What're you doing here? I thought the Bull wasn't your cup of tea."

"It wasn't, but I'm thinking that it might be now," he looked again at Judith whose pulse, impossibly, quickened further. "Who is this beautiful young lady, Thomas?"

"Forgive me. Cuthbert Burbage, this is Judith Shakespeare. Judith is our most dedicated fan, and critic it seems." Thomas gave Judith a smile. "She's been coming to our shows for months now."

"Burbage?" Judith's voice came out smaller than she'd hoped. "As in James Burbage?"

"Yay," Thomas confirmed, "This is Master James' son."

Now Judith recognized the expression - she had seen the father mirrored in the son.

Cuthbert looked around for an empty stool, and having found one, pulled it up beside the bench where Thomas and Judith were seated.

"Are you looking for your father?" Thomas asked.

"I was. But I saw him outside. I thought I'd catch a drink now. What happened to Wilson? It looked like he'd been beaten with a spade."

"He's drinking hard again," Thomas admitted.

Cuthbert shook his head.

"Judith here says it's all his fault, too, that his woman cheated on him."

"That's not what I said," Judith began defensively. "Infidelity is wrong - it is never ok. The point I was trying to make, however, is that, while wrong, there still must have been some reason for it. And reasons, deep down, are hardly ever one sided. Maybe Robert cheated on her first, for example. For all we know maybe Robert takes a hand to her. There just has to be more to it. To simply blame her for everything because the bible says women are a temptation, is, well, stupid."

Cuthbert nodded his head in thoughtful consideration. "Perhaps, but if the woman you love sleeps with another man, reasonable arguments like the one you just made are irrelevant. When you find out your love is cheating on you, passions take over, emotions, pride, shame, confusion, anger. Reasonable arguments about what led to what and who did what and who could have done what are beside the point."

"Reason is never beside the point."

Cuthbert looked at Judith and a grin crept across his face. "Then you, my dear, have never been in love."

8

Over the next several months as the cold, whipping London winter turned into a chill, damp early spring, Judith had a hard time getting Cuthbert out of her mind. When she stayed up late with her mistress, chatting and reading books by the fire, in the back of her thoughts the image of Cuthbert's dark, handsome smile lingered. When she put on her sturdy walking shoes and strolled about town buying lace or scent, she swore she heard his voice at the greengrocers' stall behind her. It was bothersome, to be honest, how often he appeared to her at night in her dreams. During the day she was able to forcibly push thoughts of him away, but at night, she had no defenses. And what made things worse was that he now showed up regularly at the Bull. Ever since that first night a few months back when he had appeared at the end of Wilson's harangue, handsome and smart in his well-fitting doublet, he'd made the Bull his new home and now he popped in two or three times a week at least. He didn't always sit near her, sometimes he even went and sat with other friends not associated with the troupe, but still he showed up at the pub on such a regular basis that Judith couldn't help but wonder if his sudden presence had something to do with her.

One night they found themselves alone together in the street. It was at the end of a long evening of drinking and talk at the Bull, when Judith should have left and walked back to the Mountjoys' hours earlier but, for some reason, hadn't. When she finally wrapped her cloak around her and stepped over the threshold of the pub into the cold night air there he was, not four feet away, his strong back and broad shoulders nearly close enough to touch. He was shuffling his feet and blowing into his hands, not aware at first that Judith was right behind him.

At the sound of her cough Cuthbert turned and faced her. In the thin moonlight their breaths caught and created a spiral of steam between them. Judith waited expectantly for Cuthbert to say something, anything, but he just stood there in impenetrable silence. Seconds passed and their fleeting chance at intimacy slipped away. The door to the pub opened again and a burly man pushed Judith aside yelling, "Out of my way!" When she turned again towards Cuthbert, he'd moved on.

As Judith made her own way home that evening she justified what had happened by the cold of the evening. Of *course* he'd wanted to get quickly away, she told herself, it'd been *freezing* outside. Only later, after she had made it all the way back to the Mountjoys' and was safe and warm under the wool blanket in her own bed, Joan snoring soundly beside her, did Judith realize that Cuthbert had walked in the wrong direction. He lived in town, like her, yet he'd gone in the opposite direction down Bishopsgate Street. Had it been a mistake? Had he some other business to attend to, at that time of night? She finally fell asleep on the hopeful thought that he'd seemed as nervous as she, and that as a result of this had mistaken his direction and walked the wrong way. She pushed from her thoughts any possibility that he might have been heading towards the brothel on Wormwood.

A couple of weeks later on a Sunday morning, Judith prepared for church. She'd taken her brother's letter to heart and after having avoided it for the first three years of her tenure in London, she finally understood that for the good of her family, if not for herself, she needed to attend church services again. The Act of

Uniformity set down by Queen Elizabeth required every English citizen to regularly attend Protestant church services on Sundays, but Judith, and indeed the entire Shakespeare family, had always been ambivalent about going. Judith's mother still secretly observed Catholicism and her father had never pushed the Protestant faith. All the Shakespeare children grew up in a house conflicted by the two main religious choices in England, and while Judith certainly believed in God and in Christianity, having to choose between the state religion and the family religion always left her uncomfortable. That had been one of the benefits of working for the Mountjoys. As a Huguenot family they were not required to obey the Church of England, and by living in their house Judith had been able to avoid joining a local parish and becoming a regular churchgoer. But William's letter warned her that the Shakespeare family was in trouble; her father was now on a list of recusants and was going into debt trying to pay off the hefty fines incurred for failing to swear true allegiance to the Protestant faith. Judith understood the subtle suggestion from her brother that it wouldn't be a bad idea if she affirmed the Shakespeare name in London, at least, and showed up regularly in church.

So after pinning up her hair, putting on a clean gown, and walking the few blocks north to the parish church, Judith entered the sacred building and settled in a back-row pew. She sat quietly through the long hours of the service, her head down, her missal open before her, trying to pray but, as usual, outside thoughts running through her head. Mrs. Mountjoy had recently acquired a precious, leather-bound volume of Henricus Agrippa's Declamations and they'd spent the past week gripped in a feverish deciphering frenzy, reading and rereading the Latin text together. Judith simply could not believe that a man would write a book about all the reasons woman was actually the superior creature. Drinking claret and eating biscuits late into the night, Mrs. Mountjoy and Judith giggled like children as they read that woman was superior to man because she was created by God in paradise, while man was created outside of paradise and brought in. Or, that woman was superior to man because God made her from better raw material; Eve was formed from a purified substance, while Adam was created out of nothing but vile clay. Judith had to go back and reread portions of the bible to see if these interpretations were actually correct, but she found nothing to contradict them. Judith's favorite argument of Agrippa's, by far, was that woman was superior to man because she sinned only in ignorance, while man had sinned in knowledge. And in fact, because Adam was the worse sinner over Eve, that was the reason why Christ took the form of a man, and not a woman.

Judith was so engrossed turning over these novel arguments in her head that she hardly noticed when the service ended. Suddenly everyone stood up around her and she scrambled to get herself together and shuffle towards the exit with the rest of the crowd. Her knees hurt from the hard wooden prayer bench and her head ached from all the incense, but it had been another successful morning of thoughtful contemplation and Judith felt content. She almost appreciated going to church; it was a good place to think. As the crowd moved forward out of the pew Judith was startled out of her placidity by the sight of Cuthbert ahead of her, already making his way down the middle aisle. How could she have failed to notice him before? She rubbed her eyes to make sure it was really him, that she wasn't imagining his presence as she did nearly every day on the street, but no, it was him alright, dressed up quite fine in his Sunday best.

Judith evaluated her own worn skirts and simple shoes and felt disheartened. She wished she'd had time to clean her shoes properly, or at least borrow a better gown from one of the other servants; this one was many years too old, and now a bit short for her as well. Judith patted the pins in her hair and stuffed the loose strands into place. Walking out of the pew she stumbled and caught herself on a heavy wooden aisle marker and her hand left a humid, wet palm print behind. As Judith neared the exit of the church, everything happening much too quickly, she felt a hand grip her by the elbow. She looked around and found Cuthbert himself pulling her out of the main throng of churchgoers and into a small recess of the building.

"I didn't know," he said, his dark eyes alight, "that you were a member of this parish."

"Yay. I am. I come regularly."

Cuthbert looked at Judith inquisitively, but she ignored it.

"Of course," he said in a lowered voice, seeming to understand, "there are so many people here, 'tis hard to know who's always in attendance and who isn't."

Judith looked at him gratefully and for a moment their eyes locked.

"You look beautiful today," he said, close to her ear.

Judith's heartbeat quickened. The sounds of the other churchgoers exiting the building receded from her awareness.

"Are you here by yourself?"

She nodded. "The Mountjoys don't go to this church."

"Of course."

"Are you?"

"Am I what?"

"Here by yourself?" Judith realized for the first time that Cuthbert was not perfectly composed either.

He shook his head. "Nay. But I told father and mother and the rest of the family to go on ahead. We usually separate after church anyway, they go home and have a big dinner and I tend to go for a long walk around London. It's a good time to think."

Judith nodded.

"Would you like to take a walk with me?"

Judith nodded again.

Over the next couple of weeks it became a regular thing, Sunday walks together after church. They never acknowledged each other before the service, or sought out each other's eyes during it, but after the service was over and the last congregant had filed out of the building, Judith and Cuthbert met up a block away and strolled together for hours around the perimeter of London. They avoided the busiest streets and often lingered in the much less populated Southwark district, the unstated but understood objective being not to run into anyone they knew. It was a treasured time for both of them, away from the preening eyes of the Bull patrons and the Leicester's Men, away from family, responsibilities, expectations.

Judith learned that Cuthbert loved archery and games of skill and that as a child he'd gotten into trouble for making a slingshot out of a discarded codpiece. Cuthbert discovered that Judith adored marchpane and sugared plums and that in the garden in the back of her Stratford house she'd given all the flower bushes names, like Charles, Robert, and Elizabeth. He imagined her skipping about the lilies, snapdragons, and marigolds as she described for him the games she used to play there.

It was during one of their Sunday walks that Judith finally unlocked the mystery as to why Cuthbert wasn't more involved with the Theatre. She knew that James frequently offered Cuthbert performing roles in the ongoing shows, and a hand at managing the company books, but Cuthbert was always firm in his refusal to get involved.

"I saw what it did to my mother when my father abandoned his trade," he told Judith, hesitating for just a moment over the revelation. "For years we were very poor. We didn't have proper clothes. We didn't have enough to eat. I used to scramble for scraps in the waste thrown out by the Angel." Cuthbert grimaced at the memory, but went on. "My father was always gone at nights, trying to gather an acting troupe together and searching for profitable places to perform. I was left to comfort my mother and take care of her in his absence. My younger brother doesn't remember the hard times. I never want to go back."

Judith looked at Cuthbert and saw for the first time the thin lines etched in the corners of his temples, the dark expression of pain reflected in his eyes. Her heart went out to him. Cuthbert wasn't all teasing and games, she realized, he was a man with a history and he'd been hurt and disappointed in the past, just as she had been. Judith understood the desire to avoid returning to a difficult place, but at the same time, she had a hard time understanding how Cuthbert could keep himself away from the Theatre. It was such a wonderful place.

"If I could, I'd spend all my time at the playhouse, every day of every week," she admitted.

Cuthbert looked at her curiously.

"I spent much of my childhood writing stories and playacting in the forest with my brothers and sisters. The best times of my life were attending the shows that came to Stratford with the traveling troupes."

Cuthbert noted Judith's enthusiasm, the way it made her blue eyes brighten, her smooth cheeks bloom a shade of red. He was drawn, in some inexplicable way, to her innocent energy and excitement.

"I'd give anything to have the chance to work for your father. To work for the Theatre."

But Cuthbert shook his head. "As a boy I vowed that as a man I would never be poor. And I've been working towards that goal ever since. No one will ever get rich working in a playhouse," he said disparagingly. "The only sure path to wealth is through the nobility."

Judith nodded, not sure she actually understood, but she let him continue.

"My apprenticeship to the wealthy gentleman Cope was the first step. Through him I've met so many other well-connected people. He has dinners nearly every week with twelve, fifteen, even twenty guests at a time. You should see some of the robes the men wear, and the jewels the women wear. Long dripping pearl earrings that are so heavy they make the earlobes sag!" Cuthbert touched Judith's ear lightly, imagining her dressed in jewels. "He travels all around England, securing export deals and attending court. It's only a matter of time before he introduces me to a wealthy, lonely dowager."

The revelation tripped Judith up. For a moment, she didn't know what to say. She was afraid to find out that Cuthbert was serious, that he was really looking for an opportunistic marriage that was just about money. "Really?"

"Oh, well, no, ha ha, dowagers are never any fun," Cuthbert said, trying to recover himself. After a moment he stopped, bent low, and picked a handful of daisies from the field beside their path. He offered the bouquet to Judith, his head bowed, his arms thrust out before him in mock supplication. "In all the time I've worked for Gentleman Cope, however," he said, glancing up at her with his dark brown eyes, "in sooth, I've never seen a guest as beautiful as you."

A frightened look crossed Judith's face as he offered her the flowers, like that of a rabbit cornered by a wolf. It passed and Judith accepted the offering. They resumed their conversation from somewhere before where he'd mentioned the wealthy dowager and Cuthbert failed to notice when, a few minutes later, Judith quietly let the flowers slip from her hand and drop to the ground.

At the end of their walk that day Judith returned to the Mountjoys' with a queasy feeling in the pit of her stomach. As if something weren't quite right any longer. Later that evening, after her duties were done and Judith was allowed some time to herself, she brought out the clean paper from underneath her bed and began to write a new play. It was a love story, and for the first time, Judith's heart was wholly in it. She set down the first sentence, "Two households, both alike in dignity..." and the rest of the writing came easily. In the back of her mind no longer was there any secret disdain when her characters acted irrationally or confusedly out of passion. The male protagonist was a boy named Romeo, from a good family and of a good character, but coming from a line of devoted Protestants. Faith was paramount in his family's traditions and from an early age his mother had ingrained in him the belief that only Protestantism held the one true moral code. The female protagonist was a young girl, Juliet, also of a good family and having a modest nature, but this time stemming from a long line of devoted Catholics. Her family too centered most of its identity around its faith, and had a strong dislike of anything and anyone not Catholic. Judith added for Juliet the character of a rotund, talkative maidservant who walked around the house holding rosary beads and saying prayers before every slight task. It was her first good transformation of Joan into a likeable character.

Judith scribbled on. For years the two families, despite living side by side in the same village and on neighboring streets, feuded. Members of each family were killed in duels over inconsequential slights, and even simple trips to market were marred by slurs and insults. While good people individually, the problem was that both families on the whole were certain they were right, that they followed the one true faith, and that the other family was not just wrong, but unforgivably blasphemous. In such a heated stew, the two young people met and fell in love.

Judith found it easy putting to paper the fantasies she'd dreamed up over the past many months of Cuthbert declaring his love for her, with the heated embrace that always followed. She also wrote knowingly about the torment of trying to stay apart, when every piece of your flesh wanted to run without hesitation towards your lover's embrace. For Romeo and Juliet the days passed and the nights stretched to eternity with unrequited love and the longing not to be forced apart.

At this point, for the first time in her writing, Judith paused. She leaned back in her chair, rubbed her sore fingers, and looked out the window. What *was* the future of this promising young couple? She was having a hard time picturing it. All goes well and their marriage brings the two families together? Their parents find out about a marriage plan and in the nick of time prevent it? The two run off together and disappear into the forest? Judith couldn't tell what ending felt right; what ending made the most sense. For her and Cuthbert's sake, she wanted to believe that all young lovers were eventually destined to be together, but she couldn't help pausing, knowing that this was naive, that sometimes things didn't work out the way they should. Mrs. Mountjoy would tell her, she knew, that love never worked out. Disheartened and sad Judith put down her quill and stopped writing. She would have to figure out the ending later. She continued to sit at the desk, staring out the window. After a few more minutes of contemplative reflection Judith picked up the quill, took out a fresh sheet of paper, and began writing a reply to her brother.

Dear William,

I can not express what a lovely surprise it was to receive your letter. I am still smiling over it, and have reread your words at least a dozen times. I'm pleased to be able to inform you that I'm healthy, happy, and still corn-stalk blonde. The Mountjoys' are also good people to work for, fair and honest, and kind in every way. London is a fantastic place to live. It can get a bit crowded and noisy in the daytime, and it doesn't have as much open space as back home, but it is such a lively city, with such a loud and strong heartbeat. You would enjoy it here, I am certain.

What did you end up deciding about the scrivener's apprenticeship? Are you still in school, or have you left? I understand the difficulty of the choice, but let me say that, if resources permit, I think you should stay in school. For how much longer will you be able to spend your days reading Ovid and learning history? For how much longer will youth last? I envy you the freedom from certain responsibilities that youth allows. At the same time... if I am to be honest, while the decision was abrupt, I am quite glad to be in London and grown up out of my own youthful circumstances. While I sometimes tire of the chores I am required to do, I revel in the freedom I am allowed here to discover my own destiny.

Rest assured, I now attend church regularly. Your letter reminded me not to be remiss in my duties to God and so with a humble heart I go to the parish church every Sunday and sit for services. Often, I pray for our father and mother, and little Anne too whose passing still pains me.

I must also share with you, little brother, for I am sure you'd understand, the news of my new friendships. Not long ago I went to a stage performance of the acting troupe the Leicester's Men, and ever since then I've made it a habit to go back as often as I can. But even better, I spend time at the pub afterwards with the members of the troupe, talking, laughing, and discussing the plays. I have made so many good friends here, I wish you could meet them all... If you ever come to London, dear brother, I would have a great time introducing you around to men I am sure you'd have a lot in common with.

Finally, I can not keep back with you, I have begun trying my own hand at writing plays. Sort of like the things we used to perform in the forest and at home for father, but much more serious. It's rather difficult, in fact, to write a real play for a real stage and a real audience! I've included in this letter a few of my initial attempts so you can see... what do you think? I greatly value your opinion and impressions on the matter.

Please give my love to mother and father, and tell them that I am well. They have been good, wise parents, and I appreciate that now even if I didn't always before.

Your Sister,
Judith

Judith considered telling her brother about Cuthbert, but she couldn't find the right tone or the right words, so she didn't. Instead, she got out her old scraps of plays, reread them one by one, and then carefully folded them in with the letter to her brother. She hoped William liked her ideas; she was certainly anxious to learn his opinion. The only draft she kept aside was the one she was currently working on about the lovers Romeo and Juliet. Until she could figure out the ending, she wanted to keep that one by her side.

9

The following Sunday after church Judith made her way to the rendezvous spot with Cuthbert a few minutes early and was able to watch as he approached from down the street. His gait was confident and swift, his stride purposeful, and he didn't seem distracted by the sounds or activities on the street around him. Even from a distance Cuthbert looked handsome, his thick brown locks bouncing on his smooth high forehead. As he got closer Judith saw that he was carrying a small rectangular box.

She raised her eyebrows and pointed to the item.

"You have the eyes of a fox," Cuthbert winked. "I was trying to keep it hidden in my sleeve, but I see you've noticed my surprise."

Judith's heart skipped a beat as Cuthbert withdrew a present from underneath his arm. He offered it to her with a swirl of the hand.

She smiled and took it.

"A trinket. For our walks together." Cuthbert started to say more, but then decided it might be wiser not to tell Judith that the gift was actually a cast-off of Mistress Cope's.

Judith wondered if it was a courting gift, but the first courting gift was traditionally a ring and the box was too big to be holding a ring. She lifted the lid and found instead a feather fan, like the ones all the fashionable ladies were now carrying about town. Mrs. Mountjoy had acquired one quite like it from Venice just the week before. Judith lifted the delicate feathers from their velvet-lined bed and spread open the folds. In the center of the handle was a mirror that glittered and shone in the sunlight. Judith laughed as she looked at her reflection.

"Shall we?" Cuthbert asked, holding out his arm. "I'm ready to get out of the city."

As they walked in comfortable silence out past the busy streets of London, Judith took pleasure in the weight of the gift resting in her hand. She'd never received a present as thoughtful, expensive, or pretty as this one before, and it was a gift she knew she'd keep forever. Unlike the rabbit pelt she'd gotten as a child from her father once and ruined. She recalled how soft and fluffy the pelt had been, kind of like the feathers of the fan. For months she'd carried it everywhere with her, to the table during meals, to the tub when it came time to wash, even under the blankets in bed at night, until it had disintegrated in her hands, the skin having grown thinner and thinner until she picked it up and the overworn fibers literally pulled apart and fell away in her grasp. She'd cried for hours before burying the remnants of the pelt out in the garden. Judith thought about where in her room at the Mountjoys' she could safe-keep this present, away from Joan who, if she discovered it, would certainly play with it and abuse it.

"I gave my mother a fan once," Judith recalled after a moment.

"Did you?"

"I couldn't have been more than seven, eight years old. I spent hours collecting chicken feathers from the field behind our house. I wanted only the good ones, you know, nothing bent or broken, and you'd be surprised how hard it is to find good whole, clean feathers."

"I'm sure," Cuthbert agreed.

"When I finally had enough of them I carefully tied the feathers together with string I'd dyed myself." Judith grinned at the memory. "I was so proud. I thought it was the prettiest thing I'd ever made. I was sure, with this present, that my mother would finally love me."

"All mothers love their children," Cuthbert said, with a certainty borne of secure maternal affection.

"Nay, yay, I suppose," Judith looked again at the gift in her hand. "Anyhow, it turned out that my mother didn't like the fan. She thanked me for it, of course, but she never used it and I never once saw her with it. I always wondered what became of it." Judith was surprised at the pain she felt relating this memory all these years later.

The story reminded Cuthbert of how his mother idiotically saved everything he gave her, even an old chipped die he'd found playing in the street as a child. It'd been so worn its sides were barely legible and one edge had cracked off, but Cuthbert had been sure, as all seven year old boys are, that the mysterious die had magical powers and he'd said as much when he gave it to his mother. The good woman kept it for years in the drawer of their writing desk, and for all he knew, it was still there, tucked away in the back by the used matches and nubs of sealing wax.

Cuthbert and Judith slowed their gate as they reached a field on the outskirts of London. In the distance a couple of archers practiced their aim on targeted hay bales, and even farther out a group of horsemen could be seen traveling south. Every so often the wind carried the cries of the archers' success far across the fields. Cuthbert turned to Judith and took her hand in his own. He ran a finger along the dainty white scar on the inside of her palm that she'd gotten learning how to iron. It was the only mar he'd yet discovered on her otherwise perfect frame.

"Maybe we should sit down," Judith said, instinctively pulling her hand away. They found a copse of poplar trees a few yards off and Cuthbert cleared a spot on the ground for them free of brush and rocks. His movements were slow, methodical. He seemed to know what he was doing and Judith easily followed him.

It'd been a mild day, the sun bright and shining but the full heat of summer still struggling to arrive. Judith had felt slightly cold all afternoon, but with Cuthbert's close presence and the soft fan in her grip a new warmth enveloped her. They sat down and Cuthbert took up her hand again, this time pushing her sleeve up past the elbow so he could stroke her skin from the tiny white scar in her palm up past the soft curve of her arm. The heat spread into Judith's shoulders and neck. She leaned back, closed her eyes, and rested against a tree. When she opened her eyes again a few minutes later everything had come into focus, the birds hopping in the trees, the leaves rustling in the wind, the fact that she and Cuthbert were meant to be together.

Because she loved him. Yes, she was ready to admit it now, she loved Cuthbert Burbage. She'd been afraid to acknowledge it because of everything Mrs. Mountjoy had warned her about, about how love captured you and turned you into a desperate animal, about how love ruined your senses, confused your mind, upturned your reputation. But there was no denying it. Judith didn't have a choice any longer, she was too deeply along.

Mrs. Mountjoy had also warned her about the fire of a man's touch; that there was nothing else that made you feel so alive in the entire world. At last, Judith understood. With every inch of her being the only thing she wanted was to pull Cuthbert close. She shivered the length of her body and turned her head to look at him. His dark eyes were focused on her arm and he seemed intent on watching her skin react to his touch. When he finally noticed her watching him his eyes softened and a smile of mutual knowing crept across his face.

Cuthbert had been trying not to touch Judith for weeks. He'd been attracted to her from that first day in the pub, of course, and he'd known from the beginning that he could easily have had her, but he'd been doing his best to hold back and treat Judith differently. He'd never met anyone quite like her before, so beautiful, so innocent, and at the same time so sharp and witty. She was surprisingly enjoyable to be around. He'd never stopped to imagine where their friendship might lead, if not this. He'd been trying to hold back because he knew deep down that there was no real future in their being together, and for once, he cared enough about the girl to acknowledge that. If only Judith were wealthy, Cuthbert groaned inwardly, pressing her arm more firmly, or at least a good Protestant. His mother would never stomach his marrying a Catholic. Neither would his father, for that matter, and his father cared so little about what he did.

Judith drew her hand away from Cuthbert's and reached up to stroke his hair. It was as soft and thick as she'd always imagined.

Cuthbert leaned in and kissed Judith lightly. She took the measure of his moist, warm lips and tried to memorize them for a story she knew she'd write later. Pulling away, Cuthbert admired Judith's fair skin and tousled hair and then decided to give in to his desire. He leant forward and kissed Judith again, this time with urgency.

Judith's body responded in a way she'd had no idea was possible. She felt taken up, like a rowboat on the mighty Thames, rising higher and higher with the gathering waves of a storm. Cuthbert shifted so he lay lengthwise on the ground next to her and with an expert heave of his arm repositioned Judith so that she lay firmly beside him. Judith had never known a happiness like this before, she'd never known such comfort and warmth and she was grateful Cuthbert wanted to share it with her, only her. She remembered calling down a deep, dark, abandoned well once as a child, and how, after a suspended moment, a ping had actually come back to her. It'd made her feel so much less alone in the world.

Cuthbert was aware of Judith's soft sighs, of her silky hair, her cool skin. He worked to lift her skirt with one hand while trying to untie the top of her bodice with the other. He was able to open the bodice first and quickly he grabbed a hold of her soft, warm breasts.

The contact of Cuthbert's rough fingers on her sensitive skin shot through Judith's consciousness like an arrow. The birds stopped singing and the sun became unbearably hot. Judith glanced down and saw her bodice open before her, Cuthbert's hand digging around inside, and felt considerably shamed. She wanted to be with Cuthbert, more than anything, but not like this. Judith pushed Cuthbert away and struggled to sit up.

"What? What 'tis it?" Cuthbert asked, disappointment tinged with something harder edging his voice. He looked around, expecting to see a prurient stranger or something else unwelcome as the cause of their interruption.

"Not now, not like this."

Cuthbert was still confused.

"Forgive me," Judith said, turning away, "just not like this." Her fingers shook as she retied her bodice.

Cuthbert let out a tick of exasperation. Judith had been so perfect in so many ways, but in this, she turned out to be just like all the other women. She wouldn't submit to pleasure without a lot of pleading, or coin, and at the moment Cuthbert wasn't interested in giving her either. He'd thought she was happy enough with the fan.

That afternoon Judith returned to the Mountjoys' to find that another letter had arrived from her brother. They were writing to each other more frequently now, nearly every other week, and his observations and gossip were always entertaining. With a tinge of anticipation Judith took the thin epistle up the stairs and opened it while lying on the bed, her feet hanging off the side of the frame.

> *Dear Sister,*
>
> *Your last letter arrived with perfect timing. Baby Edmund finally began talking and out of joy I shared your letter with him - I hope you don't mind. He enjoyed the little story you included, so I went back and read him all the other ones too. I promise, I'll comment on them myself in a minute, but know that Baby Edmund is already a fan. His favorite right now is the one about the stranded duke. After I read it to him he gurgled and spit and with a fist raised in the air shouted something remarkably close to "Juuee" - which I took as due recognition of his big sister's name, though Gilbert tells me he might have been wanting more berry juice.*
>
> *Anyhow, you can not imagine the commotion it caused around here when Baby Edmund at last began talking. He's going on four years now, and before last*

week, nothing but gurgles and moans and incantations to the fairies. Father's been considering a call to the doctor, but Mother kept insisting that her boy would speak when he was good and ready and that we should just leave him well alone. It was smart Joan who went and simply fetched the doctor herself, leading him home by the hand late in the evening after supper, none of us having noticed she was even gone.

What the doctor did next is the amazing part. After looking Baby Edmund over he ordered up some milk warmed by the fire. When we brought it to him he added two little drops from one of those mysterious dark vials in his bag and the milk sputtered and bubbled like a witch's brew! Then, slowly, with Baby Edmund squirming the entire time, the doctor poured the mixture down into his ear and held him there for five long minutes. When he tipped Baby Edmund back over the milk poured out like a soupy river and with the flow emerged a yellow-gray chunk of wax bigger than you'd have thought possible in a baby boy's ear. Apparently he wasn't talking because he couldn't hear! After his one ear stopped oozing the doctor flipped Baby Edmund over and did the same thing on the other side. When it was all over your brother was transformed. At first, he was calm, as if he could suddenly hear God's own voice, and with wide eyes he looked at all of us and listened to all of us as if for the first time. Since the doctor's visit he's been running around the house with renewed energy, listening to everything we have to say and even starting to mumble back. 'Tis a wonder. It almost makes one want to be a doctor. If it weren't for those ridiculously long black cloaks, I might actually consider it.

However, the decision's been made. I have at last chosen to take up the scrivener's apprenticeship I told you about when the school year ends at Whitsuntide. I know it means I'll be leaving my studies early and I know you advised against that, but Anne - the girl I told you about whose father recently died - thinks I would make a smart lawyer. She says I have a way with words. And she seems to know me so well - I trust her opinion obsequiously (Gilbert and I made that one up the other night - do you like it?!). I suppose I can be honest with you, dear sister, and admit that I have been spending rather a lot of time with Anne and her brother Bartholomew lately. They're trying to keep the farm going after their father's death but the amount of work is beyond them. I've been going over and helping out as much as I can, clearing the fields, feeding the animals, fixing barn doors. (Can you believe it? Me, handy with the carpentry tools?) Anne seems to think I can do anything and, with her unwavering belief, at times it almost seems that I can. I read her a few of your stories the other day as we sat in the long grass after lunch, and she liked them well enough. She even disagreed with me that they sounded rough and unfinished.

On that note, I suppose 'tis about time I gave you my opinion of your stories. I'm sure you've recognized by now that I've been avoiding commenting on all the things you've sent me, and I'm sorry for that. I haven't meant to leave you in suspense so long, I only wanted to let them sit for awhile before I said anything. Because I do want to offer support, and I do like some of your ideas, but in all honesty, I just don't think you should be spending so much time and effort on them. Many of your stories are sweet, entertaining even, but remember that in the end they are just silly diversions. You should be worrying about your embroidery and cooking skills, not your writing talents (I know that sounded frighteningly like mother, but 'tis true). Only recently have you come to the vocation of writing and your stories right now seem - how shall I put it? - not quite whole, unpolished. Maybe you just need practice, but I wonder. Can a woman truly understand and write about such things as valor, honor, spirit, pride, and yes, even love? If it were just that your plays were rough, I'd tell you to keep working on them, but I'm afraid more effort would only be a waste of time because, as a woman with a limited life experience, how can you really know about these things? How can you write about them with passion when they aren't a part of your humors? Forgive me for being so blunt, but I've decided that this is what I believe. And I've also decided to tell you the truth. Your stories are very sweet, dear sister, but they shouldn't be a focus of your life (I can't believe how many you've sent over the last few months!). They can never be as fulfilling as a husband, child, and family. When I look into Anne's eyes, I know this to be true. I hate to admit it but in this, mother seems to have been right.

The good news is that spring has arrived, and summer - our favorite season - is just around the corner. The warm weather and blue skies always used to bring a smile to your face, I remember, so make sure you enjoy it. Please don't be angry with me for my forthrightness. One of these days I'll make it to London, I know it, and when I do we can enjoy pleasant days in each other's company again, maybe even by reading a book together along the banks of the Thames, like we used to do along the banks of the Avon. Until then,

Your constant brother,
William

Judith let the letter slip from her hand and fall to the floor. She closed her eyes and curled into a ball on the bed. Today, she thought, was not going well. First Cuthbert, and now this. When sorrows came, they came in battalions. Judith wished it were possible to start one's day over again. She wished it was morning and she was just waking up. She'd put on a different dress, pin up her hair instead of braid it, go to church but sit in a different pew.

Then when Cuthbert leaned over and tried to kiss her, she'd kiss him back, but only very lightly and without the passion she'd given way to earlier in the afternoon. She'd laugh and talk and distract Cuthbert and together they'd go on their way as they always did. She wouldn't let anything progress like it had somehow done that afternoon. She knew she'd made Cuthbert angry for pulling away, but he must have understood. He couldn't possibly have wanted to be with her, like that, right there out in the open, in the dirt. Judith rolled onto her stomach and buried her face in her hands.

Her little brother, it appeared, was having amorous liaisons as well. He hadn't outright admitted it in any of his letters but it was obvious he was falling in love. He spoke of this Anne from Shottery so often. For the first time in years Judith wished she were back in Stratford, so she could meet and get to know this maid who'd smitten her little brother. From William's letters it was hard to get a good feeling for what she was really like. Judith pictured a dainty, pretty maid, that smiled at all her brother's jokes and laughed at all his silly foibles. She was glad her brother had found a companion, although at the same time, counting his age on her fingers, she thought he was rather young for it. Judith wondered how much their mother knew about what was going on.

William's response to her plays, she couldn't deny it any longer, had been disappointing. She'd been hoping for clear support and unwavering encouragement, but instead William had skipped over the content of her plays entirely and focused instead on why she was writing at all. One line in particular from his letter rang in her head, *Can a woman truly understand and write about such things as valor, honor, spirit, pride, and yes, even love?* Judith's initial reaction was shock that her brother could even doubt it. She'd always assumed that he knew her so well, that since they were so close in age and since they'd spent so much time together playing as children, that of course William understood her and knew her mind, her talents, and her thoughts. But it was obvious now that he didn't know her at all. And the shock of it stuck like the prick of a quill. Judith would have been more hurt, more angry and upset, if she hadn't been quite so surprised. All she could think was that she'd been gone from

Stratford for too long. Her little brother was growing up without her and he seemed to no longer know who she was. An echo of Judith's old feelings of loneliness and listlessness returned.

Eventually Judith heaved herself up and looked around the small, neat room. Joan's blanket was folded and tucked around the bottom of her pallet. Joan was good about tidying things up on Sundays, at least, if not any other day of the week. The towel by the dry sink hung limp. The shutters on the window stood half open, half inviting, half not. Usually when Judith had the room to herself she went and took the paper out from under her bed and worked on a story, but for the first time, she didn't feel like it. For the first time, writing seemed like too much of an effort. Judith thought instead about going downstairs and trying to find Joan or someone else to be with and talk to for awhile, but she couldn't seem to take the first step towards the door. She thought about sitting outside in the garden where she could enjoy the warm air and budding spring flowers, but again, it seemed like too much trouble to actually get there. Judith couldn't think of anything that she wanted to do, anywhere that she wanted to be. Now that writing didn't motivate her, nothing did.

A light knock came at the door.

"I know 'tis Sunday," Mrs. Mountjoy said pleasantly after Judith opened the door, "but can you help me? A gown arrived from France and Elise the seamstress was supposed to fit it today, but she's nowhere to be found. No one knows where she is and I had hoped to wear it to dinner tonight at Count Saarbrucken's. I need to try it on."

"Of course," Judith said, getting up and following her mistress down the stairs to her dressing room. They spent the next hour shoving Mrs. Mountjoy into her new gown with the whalebone farthingale and tight matching corset. The design was modern, wider than the gowns currently being worn, and Judith had a difficult time fitting the dress over the stays at the waist without having the material bunch unattractively. She worked at it slowly, carefully, while Mrs. Mountjoy held onto the back of a chair. When it was done Mrs. Mountjoy stepped tentatively towards the mirror.

"What do you think?" she asked.

"'Tis nice."

Mrs. Mountjoy spent another minute preening before the mirror, then turned to her maidservant. "Are you alright, Judith? Usually you're rather talkative."

"Forgive me, m'lady. 'Tis a beautiful dress, honestly, it's lovely." Judith walked over to her mistress' jewelry box. "It just needs a necklace."

Mrs. Mountjoy joined Judith at the box and together they went through the jewels, eventually picking out a dark blue sapphire necklace with matching teardrop earrings.

"I hope he's handsome, at least."

Judith blushed red. "'Tisn't that," she said, avoiding Mrs. Mountjoy's gaze by carrying the jewels over to the dressing table.

"Nay? Then what is it that's distracting you so completely?"

"I- I was thinking about the Theatre."

"Is there a new play?" Mrs. Mountjoy took an earring from her maidservant and clipped it on. "I should go to the Theatre more, you seem to enjoy it so terribly and everyone does talk on and on about the performances. Which play were you daydreaming about now?" Mrs. Mountjoy clipped the second earring into place and smoothed a lock of hair behind her ear.

Quickly Judith tried to recall the last play she'd seen at the Theatre. It would be better to cover up that way, she thought, then admit she'd been thinking about her own plays, about what her brother had said about her writing, about how she really wished she could see her own work performed on the stage one day. But she paused too long. Mrs. Mountjoy turned from the dressing table and looked Judith in the eye.

"Tell me girl, what are you really thinking about?"

"Oh, well, I *am* thinking about the Theatre, but what I'm thinking about are the plays I wish *I* could put on there."

"What do you mean? Are you writing a play of your own?"

"Yay," Judith admitted. "I want to be a playwright. All those wonderful books we've read together, they've inspired me. And now I want to write something myself. 'Tis the only thing I want to do, in fact. I think about stories and scenes and characters all the time."

"An affair with a man would have been much more interesting." Mrs. Mountjoy teased, turning back again towards the mirror and picking up the necklace.

Judith was nonplussed.

"I'm teasing, child. It's just that, I don't know what to say. I'm rather surprised, really."

"I know now that it's all I've ever wanted to do. As a girl I used to playact at home, and now, I want to write as an adult. I have many good ideas. A number of them are set at court, and involve the Queen. Others are more historical. A few are rather fanciful to be honest..."

Mrs. Mountjoy listened as her young maidservant talked on and on. She loved Judith, in a way, and wanted to help her, if she could, but she knew enough of the world to know that Judith's plays would never make it onto the stage. It didn't matter if she had any talent, that wasn't the point. She was a woman, and a woman would never be allowed to take over a man's work. You had to work *within* the role God gave you, not try to overcome it. Queen Elizabeth knew enough of that, as did Mrs. Mountjoy.

When Judith finally stopped for breath Mrs. Mountjoy considered whether it would be better to inform Judith now, or let her discover only later, the cruelty of the world. She chose the latter. "Well my dear, those all sound like fascinating ideas. I'm glad you've found something to be so passionate about. If I can help in any way, get you a few quires of paper or extra bottles of ink, do let me know." Mrs. Mountjoy took hold of her maidservant's hand and pressed it warmly.

A wave of gratitude overwhelmed Judith. Tears fluttered behind her eyes. She realized that this was the first positive encouragement she'd yet received about her work. She wanted to kiss Mrs. Mountjoy and embrace her, but she managed to keep her place. "Thank you," she said. "Thank you very much." And like that the confidence Judith had had in herself only hours before, was at least partially restored.

10

The full heat of summer arrived a few nights later. The air was thick and heavy as Judith made her way along the familiar winding streets to the pub. A faltering breeze touched her cheek, but then it was gone and all that was left was the glaring setting sun. Judith kept her gaze on the cobblestones and thought about Cuthbert. She wondered if he would be glad to see her, the first time since their awkward Sunday afternoon encounter, or if he would pretend, as he sometimes did around their friends, that he hardly noted her presence. She remembered the fan he'd given her, that she'd used in her bedroom just that morning, and felt comforted.

There was a crowed outside the Bull by the time she arrived. Two young men had gotten into an argument over no one was exactly sure what, and now they were being goaded into a fight by the other patrons. "Clubs!" Judith heard onlookers in the crowd shout as one of the boys took the first swing. The roar of the men clutched at Judith's heart.

She stopped at a distance away from the commotion and waited, scanning the street. The best thing would be to see Cuthbert and pull him aside and talk to him privately before going in and facing their friends, none of whom knew about their intimate relationship. She waited, but after many long minutes Cuthbert still hadn't arrived. Richard Tarlton, John Laneham, and even Robert Greene had made their way through the crowd and into the pub, but not Cuthbert. Eventually Judith gave up and went inside, because if she waited any longer on the street corner she might be mistaken for a listless woman.

The next evening, the same thing happened again. Judith arrived early in anticipation of talking privately to Cuthbert, but he failed to show up. After the third night, Judith was distraught. None of the Leicester's Men seemed to notice Cuthbert's absence, but to Judith, it meant the world. Her worries multiplied like droplets of rain in an oncoming storm. She had no idea how she could find him and talk to him without giving away her feelings, but she had to know what was going on. More than a week later, after a long evening of pub talk around the usual topics of acting, women, and the thieving Spanish, Judith finally found the courage to ask James, as casually as she could, where Cuthbert was. He looked at her with a smile, knowing how much she cared for his son, but willing to pretend that he didn't.

"He's at home resting, Cornstalk. His mum is taking good care of him," James added when he saw the look of worry on Judith's face. "'Tis nothing to fret about."

"What- What happened?"

"He's a bit under the weather, been sick for, well, past a week now, but he should be fine. No worries," James smiled.

Judith nodded but her worst fears had been confirmed. Cuthbert was ill. She had a sudden image of him in bed, coughing, the pallor of his face a sickly white, like that of Anne's before she died. Judith shook the ill-fated apparition from her mind and counted the seconds to regain her nerves, but it didn't help. Things had to be serious, she reasoned, if Cuthbert couldn't even get out of bed and come to the pub. If it'd been a mere sniffle or two, surely he would have made the effort to see her. That he hadn't shown up for nearly two weeks now meant that things, despite what James had said, were serious.

On her walk home that evening Judith envisioned the Black Death coming and taking over Cuthbert's virile body. An episode of the plague hadn't broken out in London in years, but that didn't mean it couldn't start again, that didn't mean it wasn't starting again right now. No one, not even the priests, thought it had been banished forever. Judith had listened to the Puritans preaching on Leadenhall Street, telling everyone to repent and seek god or the Black Death would return to the alleyways of London. Judith wondered if she and Cuthbert were being punished for having let things get as far as they did that day in the field. She should have known better. After what had happened before, after all that her mother had told her, she should have protected things better. Judith swayed with an overpowering sense of guilt and had to stop and brace herself against the side of a building, before making the cross and moving on.

Judith hadn't ever seen a body stricken with the plague, but like everyone she'd heard the stories. She'd been told about the balls of flesh that sprouted under the arms and between the legs of victims; huge growths as big as fists that yielded to the touch and burst with pus and all sorts of bad humors. There were also the fevers, shaking, and delirium. Victims coughed up bowls of blood and within days of getting sick their fingers and hands turned black as ash. There was very little hope once a person caught the plague, and city law was that you were supposed to quarantine and abandon them. Judith couldn't imagine abandoning Cuthbert and never seeing him again. She'd always felt guilty for not spending more time with Anne before she died, for not taking more of the chances she'd been given to stay up late and talk with her through the night like Anne liked. Judith didn't want the same regret to happen with Cuthbert. While she knew it was foolhardy, she came to the conclusion that she simply had to see him. No matter the cost, no matter the risk, if there was a way, she was going to go to him.

The next evening, hours after it had turned dark and the last candle in the Mountjoy house had been put out, Judith slipped out of bed, tied a cloak around her shoulders, and snuck out of the house. The night air was cool and brisk and Judith glided through the streets of London, not pausing to observe the men sleeping in the streets, or the busy rats feeding on the detritus of supper, both of which normally would have drawn her attention.

Within minutes Judith was standing in front of the Burbages' home, looking up and trying to remember which window Cuthbert had once pointed out to her was his. She considered things from every angle before deciding that his must be the window in the upper left-hand corner. Looking around for a way to climb up to it, a vine or a tree branch or something, Judith's disappointment was acute when she realized that she wasn't in the country anymore and that there was of course nothing to use to climb up to the window. Even after years of living in London she still sometimes forgot how different it was than the country. Things were hopeless. Judith turned and leaned tiredly against the front door when, to her surprise, it yielded. Stepping backwards she suddenly found herself inside the Burbages' parlour.

It was dark and suffocatingly warm inside, but there was also a clean smell, a distinct cut of lye as if the floorboards had just been scrubbed and washed. Judith remembered Cuthbert telling her that his mother kept a sparkling house. She stood still until her eyes adjusted to the dark and then, as quietly as she could, Judith lit the candle stub she'd brought with her in her girtle. The tiny light illuminated the room, the dark wood paneling, the pegs on the wall, the writing desk off in the corner. To the left, in the deep shadows, Judith glimpsed a set of steps. She walked over to them, her weight shifted forward on the balls of her feet, her breath held tightly. She listened, but heard nothing, and so continued further into the house.

The wooden steps were old and worn and many of them creaked as she made her way up the stairs. Once on the second floor Judith stopped for a moment to orient herself. In front of her was a small window, one of the windows she'd seen from the street. Cuthbert's, she finally decided, had to be more to the right. The other direction held a hallway inauspiciously consumed by shadows. Crossing her fingers Judith approached an unknown door to the right of the stairwell and prayed that it was correct, that she'd picked Cuthbert's room and not Master James'.

The door opened with a plaintive creak and Judith stopped midway, scared that she'd woken up the entire house. But no one came running and nothing stirred in the dark. Judith pressed the door open further - it was too late to turn back now - and when she stepped past the threshold she knew she'd entered the right room. Cuthbert's breathing was loud and labored, but it was his; the room smelled of him. Looking around Judith could make out his sword and a pile of clothes in one corner of the room. In the other, by the window, a desk overstrewn with pamphlets and papers. Judith cradled the diminishing candle stub in her hand and took a step further inside. She peered at Cuthbert's face, half hidden by blankets and buried in a simple, wood-framed bed. Relief spread through her limbs. Cuthbert didn't look on the verge of death; his cheeks had grown wan, and his forehead was flushed with sweat, but he didn't look like he had a mortal illness. She watched him for a few minutes until Cuthbert, racked by a coughing fit, sat up and opened his eyes. He raised his head to the phantom in his presence. "Judith?"

She rushed to kneel beside his low-slung bed.

"Is it you?" he asked in disbelief.

"'Tis," she reassured him. "Forgive me, I had to see you. I worried I'd never be able to look on you again." Suddenly, surprising even herself, Judith began to cry.

Cuthbert sat up further in bed. "What is going on? Why are you crying? Why wouldn't you be able to see me again?"

"'Tis nothing. Forgive me." Judith shook her head. "'Tis- 'tis only that you haven't come to the pub in weeks. And I hadn't any word that you were well. Your father told me you'd been terribly ill." Judith stopped before telling him that she'd feared the plague. She didn't want to even say the horrible word out loud.

Cuthbert's head was pounding and he was having a hard time registering that Judith had snuck across London, in the middle of the night, all the way to his house and up into his bedroom. How had she done that? It showed an impressive amount of pluck, he had to admit, but what was really going on? It was an enormous risk to take just because he hadn't made it to the pub in awhile.

"I," Cuthbert coughed to clear his throat, "I was going to make church this Sunday."

Judith dried her eyes and forced a smile. "It's only- it's only that I could never bear to lose you. I- " Judith's eyes drifted down and the words came out, "I love you."

Cuthbert was still wondering why Judith would think she might lose him. Where was he going? He had no plans for a trip with Gentleman Cope. Cuthbert shook his head, realizing that he would never understand women or their crazy thoughts and their crazy actions. Then he remembered that he was annoyed with her, and he thought she might be trying to make amends for her earlier behavior in the field. Cuthbert gave Judith a smile and patted her hand.

"Everything's fine," he said, "'tis alright." Then he lowered his voice. "You really should go, though, before someone notices your presence here. I'm flattered you came so far, I only wish I had the strength to take advantage of it." Cuthbert flashed Judith his familiar, mischevious smile, and at last she understood that everything really was alright. She knew that she'd overreacted, she knew with sudden clarity that she was foolish, coming to Cuthbert's house in the depth of the night, all alone. But in truth, it had been worth it. Judith had seen for herself that Cuthbert was well, and now she could relax.

At the pub the following week Cuthbert was still not ruddy enough to join the troupe, but Judith was no longer worried. She'd overheard that Cuthbert was gaining strength, taking walks around the neighborhood, eating full meals again. She wondered why he didn't try to see her, or perhaps send a note, but she let the thought slip from her mind. The important thing was that Cuthbert was healthy and soon she would be able to see him again. Perhaps even the following Sunday. Just thinking about it made Judith smile.

"Tell us your secret," Robert Greene teased from across the table. He saw everything.

"Secret? No secret."

"No, of course not," Thomas Clarke laughed, "no secrets here."

"She's too young to have any secrets, right my dear?" John Lyly squeezed Judith's hand, giving her a crooked smile.

"I'm sure Cuthbert has no secrets either, does he?" John Laneham stuck in.

Judith tried to change the subject. "What's next after *The Golden Ass*? Another comedy?"

"I believe so," James said, turning to Robert Wilson with a questioning expression.

"Alas, look not on me," Robert said. "I've nothing for you."

Judith noticed again that, unless he was drunk, Robert didn't like talking much. The disconnect between his rowdy on-stage persona and his much more reserved off-stage person continued to bother her.

"But are you working on something?" Judith pursued.

"Nay."

"Yay," James corrected.

"Sounds like a lover's tiff," Richard Tarlton joked, and everyone laughed.

Shifting in his seat as though the bench beneath him were suddenly uncomfortable, Robert made the effort to explain. "You know the story about Cadmus and the Spartoi?"

Everybody nodded but Judith.

"Cadmus was a mere mortal," Robert reviewed aloud, "who killed the god Ares' son. Ares, of course, was unhappy about this so in revenge he sent an army of men called the Spartoi to attack Cadmus."

"Wait! I know this," John Perkin interrupted, no longer feigning understanding. "The Spartoi were the army that emerged out of the ground fully armed and ready for a fight."

Robert nodded his assent. "When the army emerged from the ground, Cadmus at the time was just a little ways away, hiding behind a bush. Knowing they would soon find him, and not knowing what else to do, he grabbed a rock and threw it at the Spartoi from behind his cover." Robert stopped to take a sip of ale, enjoying everyone's undivided attention.

"The rock hit one Spartoi square in the head, then bounced on the ground and hit another in the leg. Finally it landed on the toes of a third man. None of the Spartoi had seen where the rock had actually come from and the hurt men, howling in pain, blamed each other for what had happened. The argument grew until the Spartoi began fighting each other and Cadmus, sitting in the bushes, merely had to wait until they'd all killed each other to emerge victorious."

John Lyly chuckled at the retelling of one of his favorite mythological stories.

"But how can a man get away with killing a god's son?" John Laneham asked. Like Judith he had never had any formal schooling and so hadn't learned many of these old tales, though he often pretended that he did. "That can't be the end of the story."

"Nay," Robert admitted, "'tisn't. Later Cadmus gets turned into a snake, and other bad things happen to him, but that isn't the point. The point is I've been turning it over in my head for a while now, and there must be many ways to trick an army of men."

"Pr'haps," Thomas said, "but the real problem is thinking of them in the moment, just as you find yourself under attack."

"Yay," agreed Robert, "and that's what makes it so exciting. Your life is at stake, destiny is at play, the world can change from the outcome of a single battle, and what d'you do? Do you crack under the pressure, or do you devise an ingenious way out?

"I've been thinking about a new play," Robert announced, the excitement in his voice growing, "about a man at court who comes under attack. Initially, he's the favorite of the king, a suitor to the princess, and a member of the Privy Council. But one day he's asked to implement a new decree, a tax increase perhaps, or something more sinister, like a plan to spy on the king's men." Robert leaned forward, knocking, and nearly spilling over his mug of ale. "Either way, in doing his job, in simply following orders and surviving day to day in the treacherous world of the king's court, he manages to get a group of men turned against him."

"And somehow he gets out of it?" James Burbage guessed.

"Yay."

"But how?"

"By throwing a rock, of course," John Lyly joked, and Robert grimaced at the jest.

"He does throw something unexpected," Robert said. "Just as pressure builds to dismiss him from the palace, or even send him to the Tower on trumped-up charges of treason, with his back against the wall and no apparent way out, he turns to his enemies and announces," Robert paused for effect, "his engagement to the princess, the king's only daughter." Robert banged his fist on the table, proud of the plot twist. "In shock, his enemies are forced to concede and indeed show deference to him now that he's soon to be so near the throne. His engagement to the princess solves everything!"

Judith smiled then, remembering Cuthbert's words that a man should never, ever trust his fate to a pretty young woman. They more often got you into scrapes, than out of them.

Robert saw Judith's smile and misinterpreted it. "What's so funny? Do you think my play is funny? Why are you laughing?"

Judith was startled. "I wasn't laughing."

"Aye, you were. This isn't a comedy, you know."

Judith looked around the table for support, unable to come up with an explanation that she knew would please Robert. She wasn't about to admit that she'd been thinking about Cuthbert and the things he said to her in private.

James intervened. "I doubt she was laughing at you, Robert. Who knows what goes on in the minds of pretty young maids, eh?"

But the deflection didn't satisfy Robert. He'd been so excited about his new play, he'd been thinking about it and shaping the plot twist in his head for weeks. He'd wanted to share it with everyone too, he'd just been waiting for the right moment. And just as he'd gotten to the best part, to the part where the man is surrounded by enemies and yet, still devises an ingenious way out, Judith had laughed. She laughed! Humiliation sparked into anger like a brushfire.

"And then what happens?" John Lyly asked, trying to get Robert back to the story. "Tell us more."

"'Tisn't fully written."

The table waited anyway.

"'Tis all there is," Robert lied, and turned away.

That evening Robert left the pub early. He took a long walk around London, going over in his head all the slights Judith had given him over the past many months. It started that first day she showed up with James, when she went around asking everybody at the table about themselves. She'd listened to Laneham, Perkin, Thomas, even William tell their stupid histories. But she never got around to asking him. And later when he'd tried to start a conversation by talking to her first, she'd ignored him completely, as if she hadn't even heard him. Her whole demeanor bothered Robert, from her slumped-over lower class posture, to her tortured cat rattle of a voice. Even her yellow hair, unkempt and often falling out of her cap, bothered him. He couldn't understand why everyone else liked her so much. She was obviously stupid, didn't know much, and she never had anything intelligent to say when they discussed Ovid, Virgil, or Euripides. She had so many bothersome habits, from sipping ale in tiny little swallows, to tapping her right foot under the table, and of course she always insisted on sitting right in the middle of the group, taking up so much room in the center of things you couldn't just ignore her. Robert couldn't take it any longer - her insolence, her stupidity, her rudeness. She shouldn't have gotten involved with their troupe in the first place. Why didn't she realize it wasn't her place? More importantly, how could he get rid of her?

The cool evening air whipped around Robert's furious frame. He stopped walking for a moment to take in his surroundings. Without paying much attention, he'd somehow walked to the Burbage residence. Funny, he hadn't meant to. Did he wish to tell James what a louse Judith was? If so, James was back at the pub, of course. And then his heart skipped a beat. He knew exactly what he had to do.

"Come in." Cuthbert's voice was low and muffled behind the door. Robert opened it and stepped inside, avoiding Cuthbert's direct gaze. He took a seat in the corner by the desk.

"Robert. What a surprise." Cuthbert sat up and smiled. He'd been reading in bed, but at Robert's arrival he closed the book and laid it gently on the ground. "How are you, my friend?"

"Well." Robert got out between tight lips. "And you?"

"Much better, at last, thank you. I almost came tonight, but mother wouldn't have it. She keeps insisting I rest one more day, and how can you question a mother's care?"

Robert could only remember his mother pestering him to work harder in the fields, whether he was sick or healthy, but he nodded as if he understood what Cuthbert was saying.

"Did you just come from the pub?"

"Aye."

"What news is there? How is everyone?"

"Perkin's got a new mistress," Robert reported somewhat mechanically. "William and Thomas can't agree on who should play what role in the next production. And of course, you probably know that your father's worried about the fights that keep breaking out in the audience. If they ever get too bad, he fears they'll be used as an excuse to shut down the Theatre." Robert shifted in his seat, clenching and unclenching his hands. "Take is good, we just keep making more and more money. But the main thing is them shutting us down on some pretext to satisfy the Puritans."

Cuthbert knew that his father had been worrying about the influence of the Puritans for some time. But personally he thought the threat was overblown. Who really listened to them? Edward Clarke, Thomas' father, couldn't even convince his own son about the need to avoid the influence of the "devilish actors," how would they convince much of the public? This threat he wasn't really worried about. "And Judith?" Cuthbert found himself asking.

"Judith?" Robert tried to act nonchalant. He placed his sweaty palms on his knees and leaned forward. "Oh fine, fine. She's doing very well, in fact."

Cuthbert was surprised to hear Robert describe Judith so positively. She'd acted so odd the other night. In all honesty, it gave him a bit of pleasure to picture her distraught at his continued absence.

"Yay," Robert cleared his throat. "She and Greene have gotten rather close since you've been gone. They walk home together nearly every night now, boisterous and laughing aloud. If you ask me, something's going on between them." He tried to smile, as if this was just mere pub gossip, all in good natured fun.

Cuthbert was taken by surprise. Robert Greene? He'd always acted more the mentor to Judith, then the suitor. And Judith wouldn't let anyone walk her home but him, he knew that.

"I have to tell you, Cuthbert," Robert continued, lowering his voice conspiratorially, "and I haven't told anyone else this, but in the dark, behind the pub, I saw them together." Robert couldn't tell if Cuthbert was buying his story, but he was in too deep now.

"I know not how Greene does it, either. First Bess Hardwick, then Elizabeth Cooke, he's so good at getting the ladies. He acts like he's their friend, their confidant, I think, and then once he has their trust he goes in for the kill, getting them to somehow fall completely in love with him. Plus," Robert added for good measure, "we've all heard him boast about being such a good lover."

Cuthbert had a hard time understanding what Robert was telling him. Judith and Robert Greene had been together? He'd only been gone a few weeks, and already that cad Robert Greene was trying to move in? Didn't he know that Judith was his? The blood roared to Cuthbert's head and he had a hard time deciphering the rest of Robert's words. He knew that he shouldn't care this much, that Judith was just another woman, yet he did. It was a point of pride for him at this stage, after all the time he'd spent with her, after all the things he'd done for her and given her. She'd told him that he was special, she'd said he was talented. Cuthbert closed his eyes and swallowed.

"I wonder where else they do it," Robert continued, "where they go to be together."

Cuthbert lay back in bed and decided that what Robert was saying couldn't possibly be true. He knew Judith. He knew how she responded when they were alone together. Of course, he also knew that women were notoriously fickle and their hearts never constant, but not Judith, not *his* Judith.

"I suppose they go to one of the rooms above the inn. I think it only costs a half-pence an hour..."

And then Cuthbert recalled Judith's strange performance in his bedroom. At the time, he'd thought her distress oddly overdone, but if in fact she'd cheated on him, it all made sense. A heavy heart does not bear a nimble tongue. No wonder she kept plodding on about "losing him" and "never seeing him again." If she'd made the mistake of lying with Greene, when she wouldn't even lie with him yet, then she had betrayed him. Cuthbert's head pounded painfully and the sour smell of his sheets suddenly made him dizzy. If Judith had cheated on him and slept with another man, Cuthbert thought, he would never be able to forgive her.

11

Judith woke a few days later with the sun shining brightly in her eyes. It was a warm summer morning, the kind she loved best, the kind that always seemed to fade a little too quickly. She stretched in bed luxuriating in the comfort of a good night's rest and recalled the evening before at the Theater. The Leicester's Men had performed a farcical show about William the Conqueror, before he became King of England, when he was still young and foolish. In the second act he fell in love with the image of a woman on a jousting competitor's shield, and for most of the rest of the play he wandered about the hills of Normandy eulogizing this fantasy woman. Judith recalled the marvelous performance of Robert Wilson as the play's roguish, potion-wielding, beard-encrusted wizard. He'd been told to interpret his character however he liked and last night he'd transformed the wizard into an energetic imp, running around the stage with more gusto and verve than Judith had seen in a while. It was as if something had awakened his inner fiendishness, and the audience too had gotten caught up in the enthusiasm, stomping the ground and clapping along with his impromptu jigs as he created spells and cast potions on the unsuspecting characters in the play. Judith wondered what it was that had made Wilson so alive the night before, but whatever it was, she hoped he kept it going for the rest of the show's performances. She made a mental note to be sure to compliment him on his skill the next time she saw him.

Judith sat up a little in bed and looked out the window. The sun was already high in the sky and for the first time she realized quite how late it was. Glancing over at Joan's bed and taking in the poorly folded blanket and empty tick she wondered why no one had wakened her. Who had helped her mistress dress and pin up her hair? Judith jumped out of bed, threw on her kirtle, and rushed down the stairs. She found Joan in the great hall, her apron a mess even though it was still early in the day. "Don't ask," she said, following Judith's gaze to the front of her skirts and shaking her head and hands. "Mrs. Mountjoy's in the garden. She wants to speak with you right away," Joan added, before turning and walking away.

Judith grabbed a biscuit from the kitchen and ate it as she went to find her mistress in the enclosed garden at the back of the house. From the doorway she stepped onto a sandy path that spread before her like the folds of a royal robe. Mrs. Mountjoy had put a lot of effort over the years into developing her ornamental garden; it was a special place, bordered on all sides by tall cypress hedges that reached beyond a man's height, and snaked throughout with sanded paths that led from the back of the house in curving directions to raised flower beds that were the center pieces of the garden. There were also a few turfed areas with benches and seats, and this is where Judith spied Mrs. Mountjoy, in a small wooden seat shaded by a maple tree at the far end of the garden, holding a fan to her face and talking to a man in a dark colored doublet. Judith walked towards them, taking the time to observe a pale blue hummingbird treading the air. As she got closer to where her mistress sat she noticed that the man with her had red hair and a pointed beard. To her amazement, she finally recognized him as Robert Greene. Mrs. Mountjoy was conversing in the back of the garden with Robert Greene. Instinctively, Judith wondered if the two of them were having an affair, but then she suppressed the thought, ashamed to think such a thing of her two good friends. And anyway, who conducted an affair in broad daylight in the garden of one's own home?

"My dear, I'm glad you joined us." Mrs. Mountjoy reached out to take hold of Judith's hand, while Robert looked on with a mischievous grin. "Let me introduce you. Robert, this is my maidservant Judith. Judith, the renown playwright Mr. Greene."

Judith let go her mistress' hand and curtsied.

"But we know each other already," Robert laughed, unable to contain the joke any longer.

"You do? Why didn't you tell me earlier?"

Judith changed her opinion. They weren't having an affair, yet, but they were about to.

"'Twas more fun playing along with the game." Robert turned to Judith. "The lovely Lady Mountjoy wants me to read your play. Why didn't you tell me you had a new one, my dear? She says you have great talent and that you just need a mentor. She's convinced that I need to give your work my undivided attention."

Judith was at a loss. She couldn't believe Mrs. Mountjoy had gone to this much trouble, contacting Robert Greene - known throughout London as one of the best playwrights in the land - and convincing him to come to the house so she could introduce him to her lowly maidservant. Judith had decided that she wasn't going to bother her friends for advice anymore - at least not until she'd completed a few more plays and gotten a little more practice - but she was touched by this magnanimous gesture by Mrs. Mountjoy.

"I am ever so grateful," she said. "It's just, only, well," Judith swallowed, "the one I'm working on now, 'tisn't ready." If she was going to show Robert anything, it would be her best work, her Romeo and Juliet, and the problem with that was she still hadn't written the ending.

"Pray, show me what you've got." Robert suggested.

Judith hesitated with a writer's misgivings. "Nay, not yet."

"How about I leave and you two can discuss it," Mrs. Mountjoy said, standing up. "My work is done here and I need to get out of the sun anyway." Mrs. Mountjoy smiled and walked away, in a timely manner that left Robert wanting more. Judith hesitantly took her place in the chair.

Cuthbert woke that morning fully recovered and finally feeling strong again. He ate a large breakfast that his mother happily prepared for him, put on a clean smock, and ventured out of the house. Taking deep breaths of the warm, slightly sour air of London that he loved so much, Cuthbert considered what to do with his day. Over the past week the gossip about Judith and Greene had festered in his mind until he almost came to believe it. He'd been tormented with images of the two of them together, in various passionate embraces, Judith's bodice torn at the neck, her smooth white shoulders glistening. But now that it was a fresh morning and he was feeling so much better, Cuthbert realized how silly such thoughts were; that they were likely the result of fever more than anything else. In the night, imagining some fear, how easy a bush is supposed a bear, his mother always told him. Of course Judith loved him, and she would never cheat on him. Cuthbert wasn't such a bad judge of character to have gotten involved with a whore. He wasn't a cuckold. All he needed was to see Judith again, hold her in his arms, and kiss those sweet lips one more time to know that she was his and he had nothing to worry about.

Turning on his heel Cuthbert decided to go see Judith that very morning. He considered briefly whether he should make such a public gesture - showing up where she lived, where she might have to explain things to her mistress and the other servants, where, depending on Master Mountjoy's proclivities, she might even get into trouble for having a male caller - but after the third deep breath of invigorating morning air Cuthbert dismissed any such reservations. Judith missed him as much as he missed her, he was certain, and she'd appreciate his visit no matter the consequences. Besides, it wasn't like he was announcing their affair in front of everyone at the pub, which would be much more awkward for the both of them, only where she worked.

Cuthbert strolled up Wood Street and as he passed the goldsmith Thomas Savage's house, with the neatly tended flower garden that bordered the east side of the property, he bent and surreptitiously picked a few of the prettiest, most lush flowers from the landscaped terrace. He divided the blossoms into two bouquets, one for Judith, and one to give Mrs. Mountjoy to smooth the disruption his arrival at her home might bring. As he continued along Wood Street he thought about the famous Mrs. Mountjoy, rich as well as beautiful. He'd never actually met her before, and as he got closer to her home he started to feel nervous about showing up at her door. Would she be angry at his unannounced arrival? Would she refuse to let him in? If that happened, would he lie and make up some story about why he had to see Judith? Maybe some story about an emergency back in Stratford?

"Yay!"

Cuthbert stopped and looked about. Could that be Judith's own sweet voice he heard? He cocked his head and listened but all he could make out was muffled laughter and some distant talking. He looked around again and realized that he was approaching the Mountjoy house from the south, and that the tall border of cypress to his left might actually be a part of the Mountjoy's property. He walked more slowly, straining to hear anything else, hopeful now that he could perhaps catch Judith outside and avoid having to knock on the Mountjoy door at all. Maybe he'd get lucky and win Judith back without having to make their affair public to anyone.

"D'you think so?"

Cuthbert stopped in his tracks; this time he was certain it was Judith. He looked around and considered calling out a witty lover's remark, but before he could think of what to say, he heard the rich timber of a man's voice, playful but strong.

"'Tis very good, yes."

Cuthbert strained to listen. He couldn't exactly make out what was being said, but he knew with certainty that he was hearing Judith's voice, laughing, alongside a man's. The blood in Cuthbert's veins thickened.

He tried to rationalize what he was hearing. Judith might be working in the garden, planting flowers for Mrs. Mountjoy along with the aid of a male servant. That didn't seem likely, but what did he know about how the Mountjoys' lived or what they required their servants and apprentices to do for them? Judith never talked much about her life as a maidservant or her varied responsibilities. Maybe it was Mr. Mountjoy he was hearing, taking a walk in his own garden and asking Judith to help him, what, carry his cane?

Cuthbert noted that the voices weren't getting any further away in range. The speakers seemed to be in one place, somewhere very near to where he stood. The tall hedge of cypress blocked his view, but as he pressed up close to it he heard more.

"Be not so shy...show me more..."

"I haven't wanted...with anyone..."

The bits and parts of sentences Cuthbert overheard were enough for him to recognize at last the male voice as Robert Greene's. When he did, his vision clouded over and his hands shook. The branches of the maple tree overhead laughed at him in the wind. Cuthbert let the bouquets he was gripping slip from his hand and drop to the ground. So it was true! He'd tried to deny it every day for the past week, but everything Wilson had told him was actually true. Judith had been unfaithful, and with that dolt Robert Greene. Cuthbert gripped the cypress hedge in his unsteady hands and tried to organize his thoughts. He'd never noticed Judith favoring Greene's attentions before. Sure, he'd seen her laugh at his jokes and offer to pour ale for him at the pub, but she did that sometimes for Laneham, and Perkin too. Greene tended to defend Judith in argument, but he always defended the ladies' position, that was his peculiar habit. Judith couldn't possibly favor Greene over himself, the man was twice his age, had half his intelligence, and was not nearly so handsome as he. That wasn't being immodest, that was simply the truth. What did Greene have except a history of rich women - which perhaps made him seem mysterious somehow? - and a quirky red beard. Cuthbert couldn't believe that Judith would do this to him, that everything she'd ever said to him on their long walks together had been a lie.

Cuthbert backed away from the hedge, stumbling over a tree root and nearly losing his balance. His sword banged into his thigh and he let out an expletive.

The voices in the garden ceased. The air hung heavy and still. After a moment a wobbly head appeared atop the cypress hedge, looking down. "Cuthbert, is that you? Is it really you?"

Cuthbert wanted to run but Judith's face immobilized him. It was still just as beautiful as ever, despite the fact, Cuthbert now knew, that deception lurked beneath its sweet-looking visage. He couldn't believe how much he'd missed her smooth, pretty face. The wench! With an effort Cuthbert forced himself to look away.

"Cuthbert," Judith said with laughter in her voice, "come around the side, I'll show you where you can step in."

But Cuthbert didn't move.

"Is something wrong?" Judith asked curiously.

"Nay," Cuthbert got out. "Yay," he seemed to change his mind. "Whore," he finally spat out. Cuthbert shook his hands as if to rid himself of a lecherous poison. He didn't need this, he thought, and he certainly didn't need Judith. She was, after all, just a woman, and there were many, oh so many, of those to choose from. Without looking back Cuthbert spun on his heel and marched away.

"Cuthbert! Cuthbert, wait! What 'tis it?" Judith climbed down from the chair and ran around the garden to the opening in the hedge. Squeezing herself through, the branches tearing at her face and arms, she continued to call Cuthbert's name. She had been so anxious to see him. She had dreamed about their first meeting once he was well again and out of the house for so long. But it wasn't supposed to be like this. Never like this.

Judith ran down the street looking for Cuthbert in every direction, but he was gone. She spied an elderly couple half a league away, doddering along arm in arm, but she couldn't see Cuthbert anywhere. He'd disappeared, just like that, after they'd been away from each other for so long already.

Judith stopped to catch her breath. She had no idea what had just happened, but an ominous feeling blossomed in her stomach.

When Judith returned to the garden Greene was standing up, looking concerned. At the kindly expression on his face Judith felt a lump rise in her throat and tears press against her eyes. She swallowed and tried not to show her emotions.

"What happened, my dear? Was that Cuthbert?"

"Yay," she nodded.

Greene sat Judith down on the little wooden chair and knelt before her, waiting for her to say more.

"Cuthbert and I-" she began, but faltered.

"We know, dear. Everyone knows. But what has happened?"

"Everyone knows?" Judith looked up in surprise.

"You two weren't very good at hiding it," he laughed. "Besides, love isn't meant to be hidden. Worry not. But tell me, what has happened now?"

"I know not!" Judith exclaimed, twisting her hands together. "Cuthbert and I haven't seen each other in weeks, because of his sickness, but the last I heard he was getting better and we were looking forward to seeing each other again. I know not what just happened, I have no idea what made him so upset. Could he still be ill?" she suggested hopefully. "Could it be fever?"

"Pr'haps," Greene conceded doubtfully. "Are you sure you don't know what upset him? Women usually have a clue, deep down, if they're honest with themselves."

Judith knitted her brows together but she really couldn't come up with anything. Her head hurt and she just wanted to lay down, out of the sun, away from Greene, in her own room where it was quiet and she could think things over.

"Fret not over it now," Greene advised. "Give Cuthbert a little time to cool off. Stay away from him for a day or two until he regains his senses, and in the meantime, you can try and figure out what has so upset him. Then, after a bit of time apart so that he misses your sweet face more than ever, go to him, and make amends. If you truly love him, just go and make it right."

Judith nodded. That is what she most wanted to do - go to Cuthbert and make it all right. Kiss his lips and surrender to his embrace.

"And until then," Greene added, "make use of this emotion. Here is perhaps the most valuable writing tip I could ever give you - use your emotions. Hawk them like a desperate street vendor for every shilling that they are worth. If you are afraid of plumbing your emotions, or, alternatively, if you dwell in them so completely you can not climb out to see the perspective looking in, then you will never be able to write anything of great value. When you are at the pinnacle of your greatest happiness, take an afternoon and write a poem. When, like now, you are a prisoner in a storm of pain and confusion, find a quill and a bit of paper and express your soul. Your best writing will come of it, I guarantee you."

After Greene left Judith went back to the room she shared with Joan and closed the door. Mrs. Mountjoy assumed she needed time to practice her writing now that she'd been inspired by the famous Robert Greene, and she was happy to let her have it. Once alone Judith lay on the bed, covered herself with a blanket despite the heat of the day, and methodically went over every single moment since she'd last seen Cuthbert. She tried to recall any small nuance, any little gesture that could have been misinterpreted in any negative way. But she could come up with nothing. She remembered her mother telling her to never question one's husband, to always do whatever he asked, and to never, ever, give him reason to doubt you. But what had she done to give Cuthbert reason to doubt her? She could think of nothing.

After an hour or so Judith looked out the window and decided that the day was too sunny for the way she was feeling. It hurt her head. She shuttered the window, sat down at the desk, and brought out the draft of the Romeo and Juliet story she'd previously hidden away. Rereading the beginning of it calmed her. Soon, she was focused on editing it, crossing out words here and there, adding pertinent sentences and stage direction. When she got to the end, to the point where she'd previously left off, she took up the quill and continued writing.

The two young lovers, intent on being together, promise to wed each other in secret a fortnight hence. Once the wedding is over, they think, what can their families say? In the full throes of optimism the two young lovers assure each other that the only consequence of their union will be to force their parents and their families closer together. Not only will they wed, but they will bring peace to their warring village.

But Juliet's parents find out about the plan. Her talkative, blathering nurse lets slip that Juliet is to meet Romeo for a secret wedding in a nearby town. Furious, Juliet's parents lock her in her room and refuse to let her leave before the appointed rendezvous with Romeo. Juliet counts the hours and waits for help, but no one comes and Romeo never learns of her distress. At last Juliet realizes that the only way out of her forced imprisonment is to fake her own death. It is risky, but abandoning Romeo at the altar seems worse. Grabbing a sleeping potion the doctor had left to help her rest, Juliet drinks all of it in one swallow and drops off into a sleep so deep it mimics death.

The plan works and the next time the nurse comes in to check on Juliet, the naive woman believes her dead. Church bells peal as Juliet's body is prepared for burial. Romeo hears of Juliet's death and out of heartache goes to join her funeral procession. He has to see her one last time, even if it is unwise to show up among her family. He knows that they blame him, and his family, for her death, and that their love didn't solve anything but only made the feud worse.

Donning a disguise Romeo joins the funeral march, but when he attempts to walk up to the coffin, to peer on Juliet's quiet, peaceful visage one last time, he is identified and attacked. Too grief-stricken to put up much of a fight, Romeo is easily slain. In his last moments he staggers up to Juliet's prone body and kisses her on the lips.

The kiss wakes Juliet, who is horrified to watch as her Romeo dies before her. Juliet's family is even more shocked to see her rise from the coffin. Ignoring everyone Juliet lays next to her dead lover's body, wanting more than anything to just hold her Romeo again. She cradles his head lovingly against her breast. When Juliet's mother tries to stop her, Juliet stands before her family like the wronged Lucretia, grabs her lover's dagger from where it has fallen on the ground, and buries it in her own stomach with one unhesitating thrust. She dies next to her Romeo, together at last, in inviolable devotion.

Judith stopped writing and wrung out her cramping hand. The ending had come out much more tragic and desperate than she'd intended, but at the same time, it was honest. As Greene had recommended, it reflected deep feelings and emotions. James might not like it, as it wasn't the "lighthearted," "funny" play he'd told her all audiences want, but at the same time, rereading the ending again, Judith could sense that it was powerful. Exhausted from the cathartic effort of channeling emotions into words, Judith gathered the sheets of paper sprawled across the desk into one neat pile, put them away, crawled into bed, and fell asleep.

12

Judith woke a few hours later to an insistent pounding on the door. She opened her eyes and saw that it had turned dark; evening had come. With stiff shoulders and a sore neck she got out of bed and opened the door.

"A letter for you, m'am." It was one of the new servant-boys from Canterbury, followed at the heels by Joan.

"Is it from your brother? Let me see." Joan tried to grab the letter but Judith reached for it first. They tussled over the nonplussed servant-boy who looked from one to the other of them before turning and quickly leaving.

"Scared as a rabbit over nothing," Joan laughed, closing the door behind her. She peered at the letter over Judith's shoulder. "'Tisn't William's handwriting," she noted. "Who else would write you? An old lover?"

Judith was not in the mood. With annoyance she thought again that Mrs. Mountjoy's amorous behavior was affecting Joan for the worse. All Joan talked about nowadays were love affairs and passionate embraces in the dark of night. Judith gave Joan a disapproving look and turned her attention to the red wax seal on the front of the letter. It was imprinted with an elegant "S," confirming that the epistle was from her family, if not directly from her brother, because Joan was right, the handwriting looked different. Who exactly had written her, she wondered, and why? Carefully she broke the seal.

Judith,

The time has arrived for you to return home. Arrange your things and prepare to travel to Stratford straight away. Your brother William is betrothed and you must be present for the wedding. We expect to see you with the next traveling party that comes through town.

M

The letter was short, but certainly to the point. Judith had to reread it twice, however, before the words made much sense to her. William was betrothed? Her heart lifted at the prospect of her younger brother starting a family. The image she'd formed from his letters of the girl named Anne (for she was sure it was Anne) came to mind - a petite, buxom, happy maid that hung on her brother's every word. She pictured the look of joy that must have spread across Anne's face when her brother bent his knee and proposed. Judith hadn't realized things had gotten this far between the two of them, but now that she knew, she was glad.

But then Judith's heart sank at the prospect of leaving London, right at this moment, when things were so precarious with Cuthbert. She needed some time. Yet she also knew that she didn't have a choice, that she had to return to Stratford right away.

There was a postscript to the letter, written hastily in what looked like an afterthought.

> *There is also good news regarding your future, I'll*
> *share with you when you return. Do not delay.*

Judith looked again at the signature, a single scrawling swoop that took her a minute to recognize as the letter M. With a shock, it dawned on Judith that her mother had written the letter. The surprise of it made her suck in her breath.

"What 'tis it?"

"My brother." Judith covered, pausing to steady her voice. "He's betrothed."

Joan let out a whoop of joy but then looked at Judith with a puzzled expression. "Little William? I thought he was even younger than you. 'Tisn't he a bit fresh to be getting married?"

Judith furrowed her brows and counted the years on her fingers, confirming that her brother was still less than a full score. "Yay," she admitted.

"Must be true love then, or," Joan cocked her head to the side, "the maid's in trouble."

"Joan!" Judith exclaimed, ready to defend her brother's honor, but then letting the emotion fade away. Her mother's postscript was preoccupying her thoughts. What did it mean, there was news about her future? Did a wealthy relative wish to adopt her? Was a new maidservant needed in a household closer to Stratford?

"What else does it say?"

Judith shook her head and tried to dismiss the question.

"I'm not stupid. I can see there's more words on the page."

Judith folded the letter and sighed. "It says I must return to Stratford. That there is news about my own future."

"Oooo, I wonder what it is. You better tell Mistress Mountjoy you're leaving. She'll be disappointed though, I can tell you, to lose her favorite maidservant before the winter season."

"Oh, I'll be back before winter sets in, certainly," Judith said, although she wondered. What did her mother have in mind for her? Judith's heart beat fast at the thought that she might not be expected to return to London again, ever. She stuffed the letter in her girtle and pushed the disagreeable possibility from her mind, convincing herself that this trip back to Stratford was a temporary one, a joyous one, for her little brother William's wedding and nothing more.

It took but a day to arrange her things and secure passage back to Stratford with a group of travelers leaving from the Wrestlers Inn on Bishopsgate. Judith searched all over town for Cuthbert before the appointed hour of her departure, desperate to have a word with him and make certain everything was alright between them, but she failed to find him. He wasn't in his favorite taverns about town, and though she waited outside the Bull long past when everyone else had left, he never showed up. At the final hour Judith wrote a letter and spilled her heart out to him in words. *I love you. Love is blind and lovers sometimes cannot see the pretty follies they themselves commit. But whatever I have done, whatever I have unwittingly said, I beg your forgiveness...*

At the bottom of the letter Judith drew a calendar and told Cuthbert to cross off the days until her eventual return to London. On a separate piece of paper she drew again the same calendar, so that she too could count down the days. Before sealing the epistle and sending it to her beloved she kissed its thick folds, and prayed that Cuthbert would be glad to receive it.

Three days later on a chilly, overcast afternoon, Judith arrived at her childhood home. She had walked from the inn on the outskirts of town where the travelling party had dropped her off, along the old familiar streets of Stratford, and now she stood outside her family's door, anxious and afraid. She wanted to step inside, to sit down and take off her shoes after the long, weary journey, but something made her pause.

"Sister!" The door flew open and William stood before her in bright colored nether hose, smock, and jerkin. He looked as though he'd grown two feet since she'd last seen him. His increasing height had come at the expense of his middle, as he was skinnier too. "Why are you just standing there? Come in, come in."

"Judith! Judith is here!" someone shrieked from inside the house. Judith stepped across the threshold and greeted her brothers and sisters who hung up her cloak, took her things from out of her hands, and bombarded her with questions while guiding her through the parlour and into the hall. Even baby Edmund welcomed her home, tugging at her hem and giggling happily. Everyone was there except sweet delicate Anne, whose absence Judith felt.

"Were you attacked by thieves and bandits?" Gilbert's voice cracked as he spoke and he blushed.

"Nay," Judith laughed, "I was with a party too big for that."

"How were the roads? Dry?"

"Yay. Good and dry."

"Sit down," Joan suggested, "you must be tired."

Stepping away from her siblings and looking around the house, Judith was comforted to see that nothing much had changed, that even the stools in front of the fireplace were resting in the same worn grooves. The only addition appeared to be a tapestry hanging a little off center on the far right wall. It was of a wooded grove with two colorful birds flying amongst the trees. It was very pretty, and looked rather expensive.

"Are you thirsty? Would you like a drink?" Before Judith had left for London her sister Joan had been wild, rambunctious, and often oblivious to others around her, but now she seemed calm, thoughtful, sensitive to the needs of others. Judith appreciated the offer and nodded. Baby Edmund tugged at her skirt until she bent down and picked him up.

"Where are mother and father?" Judith asked, sitting with Edmund in front of the hearth.

"In town," William said, taking the stool across from her. Gilbert sat in the third seat available while Joan, when she returned with the drinks, got comfortable at her sister's feet.

"Tell us about London. What is it like living in such a big city?"

Judith smiled and looked around her. She felt as though she were holding court. She'd forgotten what it was like to be the center of so much attention. In the old days, when they were children and played together in the forest, this happened all the time, but Judith hadn't received this much attention in ages. "Busy," Judith admitted, "loud. There are so many people, when you walk down the street it's as if you're pressing against a river of humanity." Edmund gurgled and Joan's expression widened with interest. "And they're all different, Catholics, Jews,

Huguenots, even a few Moors, all getting along, all living together peacefully. In sooth, it's an amazing city."

"You've seen a Jew?"

Judith nodded.

"How about a Chinaman?" Gilbert had heard from a passing traveler once about far-away Asian people whose eyes were thin as slits.

"Yay," Judith confirmed. "I've even eaten their food, a thing called 'noodles.'" The children laughed at the sound of the foreign word. "Mistress Mountjoy likes to experiment. She buys all sorts of things from the boats that dock off the Thames. Not just food and spices, but fabrics, books, trinkets, and more." Judith had always loved London, but as she described its attractions to her brothers and sister she remembered again why the city held such a special place in her heart. "Merchants and craftsmen line the streets every day selling, well, selling anything you can imagine. When the ships come in, with their imported goods from all over the world, people queue just to watch them unload, to try and catch a glimpse of the latest new thing that will come in that day from somewhere across the continent. I saw a fruit once, big and round, with spiky leaves attached to its sides and crowned on top with a head of tall green hair. It was like nothing you've ever seen before, it was beautiful, and they carried it off the boat in a glass shell, straight to the Queen's palace."

"What did it taste like?" Gilbert asked.

"I know not," Judith admitted, "they only had one for the Queen. But it was called 'pineapple,' which doesn't actually sound all that good or sweet, now does it?"

"I'd like to see the Thames," William mused, and all the ships that sail along it.

"A sight to see is the Queen's procession, especially on state occasions such as her birthday, or a visit from a foreign royal. There's music and banners and ship upon ship draped in colorful finery."

Judith regaled her siblings with stories and images of London until nearly the entire afternoon had passed. They only stopped when the front door opened and John and Mary at last returned home. Judith stood up to greet her parents, setting Edmund on the

141

floor and smoothing her skirts to neaten her appearance. Her heart lifted to see them again, but she was dismayed when she noticed the wan, drawn expressions on both their faces. The business pressures William had written her about had clearly taken their toll on her father; the lines on his face were deep, his skin had turned a tallow color, and it looked as though he hadn't had a good night's rest in months.

"How now, what's the news?" William asked, stepping forward and trying to sound cheerful.

"Not good," John replied, shaking his head and pulling off his gloves.

"There are no decent men left," Mary added, clearly upset. "Not one priest will agree to a Catholic wedding for you and Anne, with a proper mass afterwards. Not one." She fumbled angrily with the cap on her head.

"Welcome home, daughter." John held Judith's hands and kissed the side of her face. "I fear you've arrived on an inauspicious day. We're trying to plan your brother's wedding, but it appears no one will give us a Catholic mass."

"Father Style refused outright, even after everything we've done for him over the years." Mary came over and stood by the hearth. "We helped him build that barn, and loaned him our best mare that time his died in the middle of winter. Do you remember?"

John nodded, confirming his wife's story.

"Vicar Heath at first seemed to agree, giving us hope, but something has since scared him. Now he says he won't do it. No matter what we say to him, we just can't change his mind."

"And believe me," John said, "Mary's tried." The couple exchanged a look of common struggle. "The Protestants are winning," he added tiredly.

"Don't say that," Mary snapped. "We'll find a god-fearing priest, one schooled in the old ways and willing to marry William and Anne properly, I'm certain of it. We just have to look harder." She went over to Judith and absently gave her a peck on the cheek. "Perhaps we need to travel farther outside of town."

William's expression, which had slowly turned more and more downcast as his parents had talked, now looked heartbroken. "Farther outside of town? What are you saying, mother?"

"I'm saying that we aren't giving up. We'll have a Catholic wedding for you and Anne, even if it takes months to find a willing servant of the lord and we have to travel halfway across the country to do it." Mary looked critically at her eldest daughter's hair and dress. "And in the meantime, we have Judith back to help us prepare."

Judith smiled, trying not to show her devastation at the news that the wedding was not, in fact, already planned. She tried to calculate in her head how many days it might take to travel to the nearest village, talk to a priest there, and then plan a distant wedding, but her thoughts broke down in confusion. Her armpits prickled with sweat as she realized that she might be stuck in Stratford for a good long month or two, and that it would be longer than she had ever realized before she could see Cuthbert again and return to the place where she really belonged, her beloved city, the place she now called home: London.

* * *

The weeks passed interminably slowly. Judith returned to her old habits and chores around the house, waking early, eating little, helping to prepare the meals, clean the house, wash the laundry. She wrote to Cuthbert nearly every day, long letters that detailed the events happening around her and explaining to him all her complicated thoughts and ideas, just as she used to do on their Sunday walks together after church. She didn't have enough money to post the letters as they were written, so she waited a fortnight before bundling them up with string and sending them to him in batches. Every day she waited to hear back from him, but every day she was disappointed. At night she crossed off the squares on her hand-written calendar and prayed that when she got to the end of the drawing, she really would be able to return to London.

To Judith's surprise, her mother had softened in the years since she'd been in London. Mary smiled now with greater frequency and seemed to take an interest in Judith's opinions as she cooked and cleaned around the house. Mary even asked Judith to accompany her on errands along Market Street, something she never did before. Judith hoped that her mother now viewed her as a friend, an equal, an adult rather than a burdensome child.

As the two of them walked down Henley Street one day on a return trip from the drapers, Mary pointed to a new house that had been built since Judith had left. It had large oriel windows and a perfectly manicured front garden. "That's Richard Whateley's home now," she said. "Can you believe it?"

Judith looked at the house in disbelief. "Truly?" An image of poor, dirty Richard with a stolen apple in his hand and a sly grin on his face came to her.

Mary's eyes twinkled. "George Whateley finally made a success of himself in business, just after you left, trading wool. And now his son, your old friend Richard, is wealthy."

Judith marveled at the turn of events life could take.

"I had tea with Mrs. Whateley a few weeks back," Mary continued, the tone of her voice edging higher. "It's just as beautiful inside as out. They've the most wonderful carved balustrades, pewter pots overflowing with lilies, a carpet all the way from Turkey, oh, and a detailed map of the world on the wall. You can even see America on it."

Judith nodded and smiled at her mother.

"And Richard's grown to be a fine, handsome man."

Judith suppressed a laugh. If he was anything like her brother, and they were about the same age, he was lanky and skinny and barely a "man" at all. Besides, Judith remembered Richard as a petulant, slightly spoiled boy, who always insisted on being a part of the Shakespeare family games even when he wasn't invited. She couldn't help but imagine him now, an older version of the same annoying person.

"He's finished school, like William, and recently begun working for his father. Apparently he's so good at the business George trusts him with everything. Soon he'll be running things."

"He always did like to be in charge," Judith joked.

Mary gave her daughter a disapproving look. "Don't be rude," she said, "'tis unladylike."

144

Judith was disappointed her mother didn't appreciate the humor. She had to remember that while her mother seemed to have grown softer and kinder of late, she was still in many ways the same unyielding, humorless woman of her youth.

Mary stopped walking. "I probably shouldn't be telling you this. I know he's going to come and see you at the house later, but I want to make sure you give the right answer."

Judith watched as her mother, for the first time she could remember, struggled to find the words for what she wanted to say.

"Richard is going to propose," she finally got out. "And your father and I have already given him our blessing. He's an upright, handsome man, from a wealthy family, and it's an excellent match. Plus, you'll be able to stay in Stratford and be near the rest of us. You and Richard and William and Anne can all start families together. It's perfect."

Judith should have seen this coming. That tapestry on their wall, now it made sense - she could just picture her mother's delight as Richard presented it to her as a pre-matrimonial gift. The reason for her mother wanting to spend so much time with her was suddenly clear too. She'd wanted to get a feel for how her daughter would respond to the proposal. She'd wanted to make sure Judith gave the right answer.

Judith's skin burned with betrayal. First by the stupid Richard Whateley, who thought he could woo her through her mother. But even more, by her own mother. All these errands she'd asked Judith to go on - they'd all had an ulterior purpose. Deep down Judith had been harboring the hope that her mother wanted to get to know her more, wanted to be with her, wanted to become her friend and confidant and not just her overlord. But that wasn't it at all. Her mother only wanted to make sure Judith did the right thing - that she said yes to Richard Whateley and married to make the family rich.

It would never, ever happen.

Mary began to get impatient for Judith to say something. As the minutes ticked by and they resumed their walk home, anger at her ungrateful daughter grew.

"You will say yes."

"I don't even know him, mother."

"Of course you know him. That's the stupidest thing I've ever heard. You played with him nearly every day as a child."

That was an exaggeration, but Judith let it go. "I don't love him."

"How do you know you don't love him? You're too young to even know what love is. Give it a chance, you'll see, you'll love him in time if not right now." Mary turned in earnest to her daughter. "Besides," she lowered her voice, "you should be grateful someone as upright as Richard Whateley still wants to marry you, after your indiscretion with Master Hunt."

Judith recoiled. She was shocked that her mother would even bring up such a thing. She'd done such a good job over the years of forgetting what had happened, of putting it all behind her. She'd thought her mother had wanted that - to put the entire episode in a box in a corner and let it grow dust and film until it was completely and entirely obscured and forgotten. She'd thought she'd done everything she was supposed to, yet now her mother was hauling everything back out in the open into the light. Her mother was making her remember that horrible episode and, even worse, using it against her.

In an earlier time, Judith would have been hurt and saddened by her mother's actions, but she would have bowed her head and acquiesced to what was demanded. But since she'd lived in London, since she'd gained some independence and read all those books, since she'd earned Mrs. Mountjoy's respect and the good opinion of her friends, she was no longer the same person. She no longer felt so lowly. When her mother told her that she didn't know what love was, Judith knew she was wrong. It was as simple as that. In fact, thinking about it, Judith felt reasonably certain that she knew more about love than her mother did, a woman who seemed incapable of any selfless emotion whatsoever. Judith pictured Cuthbert and the hurt look on his face the last time she'd seen him. Worry not, she told him in her mind, I will never betray you. I love you with all my heart.

As they walked on Judith thought about telling her mother that she loved Cuthbert Burbage, son of James Burbage, resident of London and a truly wonderful man, but she hesitated. She didn't feel like causing a scene right there, in public, in the middle of the street. She knew her mother wouldn't believe her anyhow. She knew enough of her mother by now to know she would just dismiss her daughter's thoughts and feelings as irrelevant, or worse, insincere. Judith bit her lip and held her tongue, thinking all the while how unfair, cruel and heartless her mother could be.

Mary chose to interpret her daughter's lack of argument as acquiescence. She debated adding that Richard had promised to pay off the family debt, as well as help in sorting out some of John's bad business deals, but she didn't. She decided to say nothing more for the moment and only bring it up later if Judith resisted. For now, she would let the idea of marriage settle in her daughter's mind. It was big news. It was a lot for a simple girl to think about. Mary walked confidently back towards the house, pleased with herself for making such a good match for her eldest daughter.

When they got back home Mary changed her apron and went to prepare supper. Judith went directly up the stairs to the girls' room, disregarding calls for her to help with the meal. She tore out her reserve of paper from underneath the bed, grabbed a quill and some ink, and poured her feelings out in a play that followed the rise, and then horrible death, of an ambitious general and his scheming, manipulative, soulless wife.

13

Over the next few days Judith cloistered herself in her father's workroom, hiding from her mother and sewing dried flowers onto the headdress Anne would wear on her wedding day. She'd offered to make the tire for her soon-to-be sister-in-law, having picked up a few skills while working for the Mounjoys. With a jab she thrust the needle between the roped flower stems and thin metal wires and inexpertly stuck her thumb, crying out in pain. She bent to pick up the loose materials that had scattered from her lap and the conversation with her mother from the day before played again in her head. *She should be* grateful *someone as upright as Richard wanted to marry her... her* indiscretion *with Master Hunt...*

Usually things slid past Judith, slights from rude people on the street, insults from hurried shopkeepers, judgmental looks from prying neighbors; they all tended to fall behind her like the ballast of a steady ship. Mrs. Mountjoy had always told Judith she was quite good natured that way; that she had a rare ability to let things go. But this time the memory of the conversation with her mother was not slipping away like so much melted butter. This time Judith seemed unable to rest her mind on anything other than the shocking words of the day before.

"Judith! Anon, where are you?" Mary's voice rang out loud and strong.

Judith sighed and debated retreating further into a corner of the workroom, but she knew such evasion was useless. She took a deep breath, laid her materials carefully on the bench beside her, and stood up. *Judith!* She would have to face her mother again sooner or later. Judith smoothed her apron, patted her hair, and went to answer the call.

She found her mother standing in the hall, gesticulating wildly in conversation with a stranger. As Judith approached she noted the man's fine leather belt and smooth brown hair pulled back into a ponytail. She heard his low-pitched laugh, in support of some nervous comment of her mother's, and suddenly she knew who he was. Judith paused, not wanting to approach the pair, but not knowing how to silently retreat either. Then her mother made eye contact with her over Richard's shoulder.

"My dear, you remember your old friend Richard? Look how tall and strong he's grown."

Judith had to admit, Richard had filled out much better than her brother. He had broad shoulders, thick legs, and a dark mustache and beard that gave him a rugged, masculine look. Confidently, he looked Judith over as well.

"'Tis good to see you again." Richard cleared his throat. "You look lovely."

Judith blushed, uncomfortable not just with the compliment, but with having to hear the compliment in front of her mother. Mary acted as if the words were directed at her and giggled like a maid. Patting Richard on the arm she said, "I'm right in the middle of something in the other room. Will you excuse me?" She waited for Richard's nod. "You and Judith should catch up."

Mary left and Richard rested his gaze on Judith. He noted that her eyes were even bluer than he remembered and her skin fairer. At last he broke the silence. "Can you believe your brother? Getting married already?"

Judith grinned and the tension lifted. In some ways, it was good to see Richard again, an old friend who'd been so much a part of her childhood.

"'Tis a surprise, indeed. But he's deeply in love, and seems to have found a good match in Anne. Have you met her?"

"Nay," Richard shook his head. "She lives outside of town, and I'm quite busy most days with business."

Judith couldn't tell if this was a boast, or simply true. She was annoyed at herself for being so skeptical of Richard. "She's very pretty," Judith offered, "small and sweet."

"And wily," Richard added, winking.

"Wily?"

"You know, hooking William like she did. They say she'd been keeping an eye out for a willing lad to walk past her cottage in Shottery for months." Richard turned to look for a place to sit, but when he glanced back at Judith he realized he'd said something wrong.

"Just a rumor, of course, things they say, 'tis nothing." Richard unwisely continued. "You must've heard though, eh? Anne and her brother Bartholemew needed help managing the farm after their father died last summer. It's just the two of them now." Richard looked again for some sort of confirmation from Judith. "William and Anne are rather anxious to get married, right?"

Judith nodded.

"And they're both so young, right?"

Judith nodded again.

"Are they rushing the marriage because Anne, all alone in that big cottage with the wide master bedroom and double bed all to herself, once showed little William the beauty of her bedroom curtains?" Richard chuckled at the reiteration of how the men at the Bear described Anne and William's afternoon trysts. He thought the part about the bedroom curtains was especially funny, and he liked passing on the story. But as he did so he realized too late that Judith wouldn't appreciate the humor. "Forgive me," he coughed. "I didn't mean to upset you. It matters not anyway, in sooth, such things happen all the time." He shrugged his shoulders and lifted his hands. "People get married for so many reasons, a night under the stars is certainly not the worst of them."

Judith debated telling Richard that he was wrong, that the reason for the desperation and confusion surrounding her brother's marriage was religion, not pregnancy, but she refrained. She wasn't sure if it was Richard's abrasive confidence, or his scandalous insult to Anne and William's characters, but something about him really grated her. She tried to look at Richard and see her old playmate, the young boy she sat with so many times in the forest, but all she saw were his strong jaw and roughly carved nose and they only looked mean to her.

"Some people get married for money, for example," Richard continued, looking around again for a place to sit down.

"Money? Lust? What about love?"

"Love?" Richard's attention was directed back at Judith. He thought again how beautiful she was, her red cheeks, her wide eyes, her golden hair. He'd always been drawn to the fire that animated her from within. "Methought you'd grown out of your fairy telling days, my dear." He winked and chucked her lightly on the shoulder, like they used to do as kids.

"Love is not a fairy tale," Judith said, stepping back.

"For a man, no," Richard nodded, glad to have something to agree with Judith on. "But a woman, of course, is different. Women can never love, not like men can. 'Tisn't a part of their humors."

Judith knew that many people assumed women were lesser creatures. That they couldn't think as well as men, work as well as men, even love as much as men - she'd heard, and debated, these theories many times at the pub with the Leicester's Men - but she still got upset when faced so directly with the accusation. So many arguments wanted to rush themselves out of her mouth, in defense of the "lesser creatures," that they jumbled together instead and made her tongue-tied.

"Don't look at me like that," Richard continued defensively, "everybody knows it. Men are made of the hot and dry humors, women of the cold and moist humors, which makes them less passionate, more timid, and fit to be dominated by men. Sit down and relax." Richard stepped around Judith and went over to the hearth. He chose the stool usually reserved for Judith's father and motioned for her to sit next to him in another unoccupied stool. Judith didn't move.

"'Tisn't going well," Richard said, somewhat to himself. He realized that he needed to get the conversation around to the real purpose of his visit. "Let me try again. Nay, all I'm saying is that 'tis alright for a man to take care of a woman that he loves."

"Women can take care of themselves."

Richard couldn't help but smile. "Now that's the silliest thing I've ever heard." He rubbed his palms against the sides of his thighs. "You're arguing with me on purpose now, not to make any real point. Come here and sit down." Richard indicated the stool beside him. "Don't you want to be taken care of, m'lady? Don't you want a man to love you?"

What Judith wanted was to tell Richard that he had it all wrong, that women didn't need to be taken care of, but she knew that debating Richard would be a bad idea. He wasn't like her friends back in London, he wasn't interested in ideas and thoughts and arguments, he only wanted to be right. She considered humoring him, just letting him talk on for a few more painful minutes, but she knew she wouldn't be able to take much more of Richard's condescending tone. She walked over to the doorway. "I've a lot of work to do, Richard. As you say, the wedding is coming up, and there's still a lot of women's work to be done. If you came all this way just to see me," she indicated the passageway for him to leave the room, "I'm sorry, but I don't have time right now."

Sensing that he'd messed things up Richard made a final, desperate attempt to impress Judith. In a rush he told her about his wool trading and all the money he'd made in the years since she'd been gone, about his fine house and how bright his future looked. Judith listened, but remained cool and eventually Richard took the hint and left. Moments after he did Mary walked into the room with a tray of biscuits and ale.

"Alas, where is Richard?"

"He had some important money-making business to attend to."

Mary frowned but seemed to accept this answer and turned around, not bothering to offer her daughter any of the refreshments she'd just carried into the room.

Judith sank onto the stool she'd refused to sit in earlier and dropped her head into her hands. She suddenly felt very, very weary. She shouldn't really have been surprised at the interaction with Richard; her mother had warned her what to expect and in truth he'd only acted like most men, a little arrogant, a little aggressive, and because he had some coin, a little entitled. He wasn't a bad sort, really, but he was no Cuthbert either.

Judith yearned to see Cuthbert. Telling him about what had just happened was exactly the sort of thing they liked to share with each other. He would have understood both the hilarity, and the torture, of the situation. How she missed him. Desperately, she hoped that he missed her too. Judith stood up, rung her hands, and paced about the room. She tried to take comfort in Greene's advice that the best thing was a little distance, to let Cuthbert cool off and give him a chance to pine for her. Like a dream she imagined their eventual reunion, the expression of surprise and joy clear on his face, his gathering her up into his arms, and then after the long kiss, Cuthbert dropping to his knee and asking her to marry him. Judith pictured herself in the wedding coat and headdress they were preparing for Anne, walking to church on a sunny day with her family all around, giving herself to Cuthbert before god and the law. It was Judith's favorite fantasy, and the one she used most often to get her through the day.

As December approached, nearly four months later, John Shakespeare finally arrived home with some good news. He'd been looking increasingly haggard of late, with the difficulty of finding a Catholic priest for William's wedding and the heavy recusancy fines and monetary losses from his business deals adding up, but on a cool day in late November he burst into the house with a smile on his face and a bouquet of late season primroses to delight his wife. William greeted him at the door while Mary, Judith, and Joan emerged from the hall.

"I spoke with John Frith today," he announced. "'Tis all arranged. William and Anne will have their wedding, with a mass and everything." Uncharacteristically, he hugged his wife.

Mary clasped her hands together and looked heavenwards.

"John Frith," William said, sounding out the name. "He lives in Temple Grafton, does he not?"

"Yay. Now all we need is for you or Anne to live there long enough to make Temple Grafton your official domicile. Then nothing will seem out of order and everything can proceed smoothly."

"Thank you, father, but," William looked worried, "one of us has to live there?"

John nodded, taking a seat by the fire to warm up his legs. "For at least fifteen days."

William counted on his hands. "But then there won't be enough time for the reading of the bans. Not before Advent Sunday, and if we fail to have the marriage bans announced in church on three Sundays before Advent, we can't wed until after the new year."

"Not until well into January," Judith added, unhelpfully.

William looked dejected. "Does Anne know?"

"I sent word. I asked her to stay with her cousin in Temple Grafton for a fortnight while we arrange the rest of the wedding here." John smiled at his son, his eyes twinkling. "And I asked Vicar Firth to find a way to speed things up. He says we may be able to get away with a single reading of the bans so that you can marry *before* the new year. Worry not, my son, everything will work itself out. I finally believe that now. Come," he added, clapping his hands together, "let us celebrate. This is the first good news the Shakespeare family has had in a very long while."

That evening before bed Judith wrote a note to Cuthbert. Just a few more weeks, she told him, and their reunion would be at hand. Just a little more time apart, and soon, they would be back in each other's arms, feeling each other's embrace. She tore up the expired little paper calendar she'd been tracking the days on and, opening the window to the cold fall air, watched as the tiny pieces of paper fell languidly to the ground.

* * *

The morning of William Shakespeare's marriage to Anne Hathaway emerged out of the tunnel of night slowly and with apparent effort. Thick clouds churned and multiplied in the sky, threatening to keep things grey and overcast. Judith looked out from the bedroom window and crossed herself, praying that the weather wasn't a bad omen for the future of her brother's marriage. She watched as her father walked over to the barn to prepare the horses for the day's ride.

"Judith! Joan! Where are you?"

Joan grabbed her sister's hand and after a final check of their dress and appearance, the two girls went to answer their mother. Mary was seated at a table wrapping the bride-cakes they'd baked the night before with white cheese-cloths tied decoratively at the top. She handed her daughters ribbons from a scattered pile and directed them to weave the colorful bands of string through the knot at the top of the cakes.

"How many people are traveling with us?" Judith asked, getting to work.

Her mother began listing the names of their closest, Catholic, neighbors. As Judith feared, Richard was among the villagers joining them for the day's festivities. "That makes twelve, along with us of course. We'll be meeting Anne's family in Temple Grafton before the actual procession to the church."

William walked in looking wan and tired, but happy. He was wearing a rich new velvet doublet the color of burgundy with slashes of gold, and he was fumbling with the bossed gold buttons that dotted the front. His sideburns were long and Judith noticed that he'd grown a hint of a mustache too, in an effort to look a little older than his mere eighteen years. Anne was eight years older than William and in that moment Judith felt guilty for having teased her brother so mercilessly over the last few months about his "decade-older" bride. He'd seemed to take it well, but she wondered now at the sight of his wispy new moustache whether perhaps it had actually bothered him. Judith gave her brother a smile and he flashed back a warm, happy grin.

"'Tis late, mother. You can wrap those at Anne's cousin's house, before the procession. Finish getting dressed," he said, looking at her drab apron. "'Tis almost time to go."

Mary stood up and kissed her son on the cheek. She'd wanted to kiss him on the top of his head, like she used to do when he was a much smaller child, but he'd grown too tall for that and the best she could do now was reach up on her tip-toes and kiss him on the side of his face. At least he still smelled like the little boy she remembered, fresh grass and cinnamon. "Alright," she agreed, placing a cake in William's hands. "Take these out to your father to put in the wagon. And you two," she indicated her daughters, "don't do anything to muss up those dresses you're wearing."

The ride to Temple Grafton to meet Anne was quick but crowded, all the women piled into the wagon their father normally used to transport wool, all the men following behind on horseback. Richard stayed near the rear of the procession, next to William, and didn't try to move up alongside the wagon to talk to Judith. Judith was grateful for that. She sat immobile between her mother and sister, listening to various female neighbors spend most of the journey gossiping about the wedding procession and who would be in it, or about the new wedding clothes Mary, Judith and Joan had spent the past few months sewing. Judith wished Cuthbert could see her in her yellow dress with gold-embroidered hem. Along with the delicate gloves on her hands and the clinking amulets on her waistband, Judith felt quite pretty; she knew she looked much better than in the plain kirtles Cuthbert usually saw her wearing.

"Is that right, Judith? 'Tis your turn next?" Portly Mrs. Debdale, distantly related to the Shakespeares through some maternal link Judith could never quite recall, was trying to draw Judith into the conversation.

"Indeed it is," Mary cut in, "she is the elder child, you know."

"Yay, but 'tisn't her fault William's getting married so young. She'll just have to get married quickly to make up for it. Any plans for that?"

The older women laughed while Judith blushed. She longed to tell everyone about Cuthbert, but she shook her head instead, as if she had nothing to say about the notion of marriage. She glanced at her mother who was having difficulty herself keeping her face expressionless. Silently Judith thanked the Lord for holding her mother's tongue about Richard. A parable popped into Judith's mind about an eighty year old spinster who lived with her hundred year old mother. Every time there was a knock at the door the old mother rushed to open it, desperate to believe that there might yet be a suitor for her four score daughter, not realizing that her constant presence was itself the force that drove all the men away. Judith thought about trying to tell this story to the women in the wagon, but she knew that no matter how she said it, it wouldn't come across in the humorous way intended. Spinsterhood was no laughing matter.

The banter about possible matches for Judith continued all the way to Anne's cousin's front door. Judith couldn't have been more pleased to see slim little Anne, her auburn hair lifting in the breeze, her thin brown kirtle whipping around her legs, waiting for them outside the house. The clouds had cleared somewhat on the ride out of Stratford and it didn't look quite so overcast now that they'd arrived in Temple Grafton.

William was the first off his horse and at Anne's side. As soon as Judith could extricate herself from the wagon, she joined them. She kissed Anne on both cheeks and hugged her warmly. Anne, eyes wide and cheeks flushed, thanked Judith, but then quickly turned her attention to her fiance, who'd never stopped looking at her from the moment he'd arrived. Judith watched as her brother grasped Anne's hands in his own, and in response Anne's body gravitated closer to William's tall form. Their attention to each other was broken only when Mary forced them apart so Anne could finish dressing and William could help unload things from the back of the wagon.

By the time the musicians arrived everyone was ready and anxious to walk to the church. Anne looked perfect in the flowing burgundy gown that matched William's velvet doublet. Her hair was pinned high above her head revealing a tall neck, delicate as a flower stalk. The gloves were the perfect touch, Judith thought, a gold color that expertly matched the gold slashes in William's doublet. Before Anne was let out of the house to lead the procession to church the final thing was to put the headdress on, the one that Judith had worked so hard on and hidden from everyone's view for so many weeks. Pulling it out of the linen bag, the flowers overflowing about the metal frame, Judith heard the women around her gasp. "'Tis beautiful," Anne said. "I've never seen anything like it." Judith stepped behind her sister-in-law and secured the tire to the top of her head; from her peripheral vision she saw that even her mother had tears in her eyes.

The bride led the procession across town, followed first by a number of small children dressed up in finery and lace. Two teenage girls went next, throwing ribbons and occasional pieces of silver into the streets of Temple Grafton. Then came the musicians, mostly fiddlers, who announced the procession with quick, catchy tunes, that everyone knew from childhood. Their music rang out over the hills and fields of town and brought people to their doors and windows to listen, and cheer, as the wedding party passed. Bringing up the rear of the party were the friends and family members, singing and laughing aloud. Before she got to the center of town Judith caught a glimpse of the Malvern Hills off to her left. Normally full and green, this time of year they were brown, with thin films of snow covering their peaks. Judith had heard that there were caves deep within those hills and that, once found, a person could live in them for years. She imagined staying there with Cuthbert - running off together and forsaking the world, gathering wood, building fires, and keeping each other company long into the night.

"Whoa, m'lady. Why so quick to get away?" Detaching himself from the rest of the inebriated men, Richard approached Judith. She'd been trying to walk quickly enough to stay ahead of the men, but apparently her distractions had caused her to fall behind.

"I think I upset you th' other day. Forgive me, I meant not to. I meant to, not, do that. My pardon."

Judith's mother had always told her that men either hit you or apologized to you when they were drunk, but rarely both, and that it was generally better to have the apologizing kind.

"'Tis nothing."

Richard gave her a hang-dog look. "You know, you're very beautiful Juuudith, you always have been. From the moment I saw you when I was seven yearrrs tall." Richard tried to reach out and touch Judith's cheek, but he stumbled and nearly stuck himself in the stomach with his sword. Judith swallowed a laugh.

"D'ye like to hear how beautiful yu are? About your rosy cheeks? And diamond eyes?" he asked.

"'Tis nice, thank you," Judith said, in a manner you'd say to a young child before putting him to bed.

"What's yur problem?" Richard snapped, his attitude suddenly turning. Judith looked around to see who else was watching, but most of the procession seemed involved in singing along with the musicians. "Women are supposed to respond to compliments."

"Is that in some rule book somewhere?"

"Rule book?" Richard looked perplexed until he at last understood that Judith was making a joke. "You think you're so smart, don't you? So clever? You always thought you were better than me, better than the rest of us, better-" Richard coughed and wiped the spittle from his mouth. "You're not though. You're just a woman. So you can't be better than me."

Judith sighed. If Richard couldn't be on top, his recourse had always been to cut you down from below. He'd always been an immature, bothersome little boy, and now he was a repellent, obnoxious young man. Judith had no patience for him and, turning away, dashed into the crowd where more of the women were walking.

At last the procession arrived at the church. Its tall gray spire cut the sky overhead, its majestic tip lost in the few remaining clouds. The dirt pathway up to the church's front door had been decorated on either side with pots of dried flowers that gave color to the drab winter day. The musicians stopped playing, the crowd formed a semicircle around the church entrance, and William approached his bride.

Anne swayed in the wind as William took her hand and walked with her the last few steps to the threshold of the church. The priest waited, prayer book in hand, as they neared. When the young couple finally stood before him the old clergyman cleared his throat, straightened his declining posture, and asked the gathered crowd if anyone present could claim any legal impediment to the marriage of William Shakespeare and young Anne Hathaway. William never took his eyes off his bride as they waited through the moment of silence. In a corner, Judith saw Richard hurl a wad of spit into the bushes. Near the front of the crowd Mary grabbed her husband's arm and dabbed at her eyes.

It'd been years since Judith had been to a wedding. She could remember as a child getting excited every time another procession walked through town, and how she always wanted to run after the wedding party and her mother had to hold her back. The last time she'd actually been a part of a wedding was when she was ten years old and her mother had sewn for her a beautiful dress of orange and gold. She'd felt like a queen in that gown, and after the wedding insisted on wearing it around the house, despite her mother's admonitions. Until that horrible day when she'd tripped and irreparably stained the dress with soot from the hearth. She'd tried to clean it, rubbing the material with all sorts of lotions and soaking it in scalding hot water, but the stain had never gone completely away and Judith had never been entirely forgiven for ruining it.

Judith watched as William, finishing his vows, took Anne's right hand in his and placed the gold wedding band around her thumb. A light drift of snow came down, like a call from overhead to hurry things up, and the priest obliged. Anne rushed through her own vows, handed William a second knife to wear in his single sheath as a symbol of their newly betrothed status, and everyone was quickly herded inside the church for the private, secret Mass.

That evening, after the wedding ceremony was over and the celebration was underway at the local pub, Richard approached Judith and silently offered his hand for a dance. Judith had been leaning against the bar, watching the other guests and thinking about how much she was going to enjoy her own wedding one day with Cuthbert. The mood was festive, the atmosphere light-hearted, and Judith hesitated only slightly in accepting Richard's hand. They took to the floor and Richard, despite having drunk copious quantities of spirits throughout the day, turned out to be a skilled dancer. He led Judith around the room expertly and with care, and after relaxing into it, Judith enjoyed his strong hand on the small of her back and his firm shoulder leading her forward. It was the most fun she'd had in ages, and when the dance was over Judith was surprised to feel a twinge of disappointment.

"Would you like a drink?" Richard asked as they returned to the bar.

Judith nodded and Richard lifted two fingers to the barmaid.

"You're a good dancer," Judith admitted when the drinks arrived, taking a sip from the cool, refreshing tankard.

"I have been told that I can cut a caper," Richard said, flourishing a bow. The two friends leant back against the bar and watched as other dancers circled the floor.

"How do you like being back in Stratford? Is it as you remember?"

"Yay," Judith said, but then shook her head no. "In sooth, more has changed than I would have thought." She went on to describe the altered streets, missing trees, and repainted storefronts that had evolved in the last few years. "And your house, that's changed a little too." Their eyes met and they both laughed at the understatement. "I bet you can eat all the sugar-sops you want now," Judith said, referring to the candied bread baked in sugar and spice that Richard could never get enough of as a boy.

"Ha! That's what my mother always tells me," Richard admitted. "You know me so well. You always knew what I liked and what I didn't like, what I was thinking, and what I didn't understand. I've never met anyone who could guess what I was feeling like you."

Judith tried to interrupt the flow of words, but Richard continued.

"I've been in love with you from the first moment I saw you. Did you ever wonder why I always wanted to play in your games? It was just to be near you. I don't care about the stories, I never cared about the playacting. It was you. Your hair, your voice. I've never stopped thinking about you since the day you left for London either. And I've waited patiently for you to return all these years. Our house on Rother Street, it really could use a woman's touch. It's so big, it needs children." Without looking Judith in the eye, Richard grabbed her hand and finally said the words, the words he'd been holding on to for years, the words that alcohol and revelry had at last pried loose, "Will you marry me, Judith? Will you be my wife?"

Judith pulled her hand from Richard's grasp and berated herself for not getting out of the conversation sooner. She should have seen this coming. She shouldn't have let her guard down. "I'm sorry," she nearly whispered. "But I can not marry you."

At first, Richard didn't hear the words. He'd been nervous about this moment for so long, he'd been avoiding it, not going over to Judith's house when he knew he should, not talking to her though he knew he needed to make his case. It'd been easier to keep holding off. But now drink and dance and wedding music had bolstered his spirits and strengthened his confidence. And now that he'd said the words, now that he'd finally done the deed, everything had to be right. At last, he was going to have his woman, start a family, and make his mother proud. He was so caught up in his own fantasy that it took Richard a moment to notice the frown on Judith's face. He shook his head and focused on listening to the words that were actually coming out of her mouth. When it finally got through to him that the unthinkable had happened, that Judith had refused his hand in marriage, pride swelled in him like a torrent.

"But you can't refuse me."

"I can't?"

"Nay, you can not. Your parents have already given you away." It seemed so logical as to be obvious.

Across the room Judith saw her mother staring at the two of them. In a flash she realized that her mother had not mentioned Richard again after that one afternoon in the street because she'd assumed it was a done deal. Richard, clearly, believed so too.

"I'm sorry, Richard. I am truly sorry, but I just, can not." Judith paused for only an instant and then laid down the gauntlet. "I am in love with another man."

For a moment Richard was speechless, his mind working, his lips fumbling. Then anger took over.

"Your father owes me money, and another man or not, somebody needs to repay that debt."

Judith looked at him, uncomprehending.

"You have to marry me or I'll call in your father's loans. D'you want your family thrown into the street?"

Judith couldn't breathe. She felt like a cornered rabbit in one of those hunting games Richard liked to play so much. The world rushed in around her and the thick, hot, smoky pub air suddenly became too heavy to breathe. Judith turned away and ran towards the door, desperate for some fresh air.

The ground outside the pub was cold and hard beneath Judith's fingers and the sharp, wintry air bit into her lungs. She coughed and looked around and noted that Richard hadn't bothered to follow her outside. But her mother was there, slapping her on the back and telling her to pull herself together. As she listened to Mary's dictatorial harangue, Judith vowed to herself that she would leave Stratford and return to London before the week was out. There was no more waiting. There was no more of this pitiful longing and useless hesitation. She had to get out of this place and see Cuthbert again, no matter the consequences.

14

Two days later, in the early hours just before dawn, Judith snuck out of her childhood home and made her way through the darkened streets of Stratford to an inn on the outside of town. There, for the last of her money, a group of travelers heading south towards London agreed to take her with them. It was a miserable journey, thoughts of Richard running through her mind, worries about obligations to her family weighing her down. More than once a brusque, bearded man with dirt in his ears and teeth rotted black sat too close to Judith during their stops for food and rest and inspected her like a market fruit. At night she couldn't sleep for fear of being robbed, or worse. When the rooftops of London eventually came into view relief spread through Judith like a warming sun. She had made it that far, at least.

Judith tried to look presentable when she showed up at the Mountjoys', but there was only so much she could do with her wrinkled kirtle and dirty apron and no money to stay at an inn and clean up. In the end, she needn't have worried. Mrs. Mountjoy gathered her into the house without question and told Joan to keep her thoughts to herself. Judith had a story ready for her sudden appearance that explained how she was returning to work after her brother's wedding, and that the letter sent ahead of time must have just gotten lost along the way, but Judith needn't have worried. She was never asked to falsely relate it. Within hours Judith was settled back into the household, washed, and clothed in fresh linen.

The main purpose of Judith's return, of course, was to speak with Cuthbert. Now that she was so close to her desired objective, however, she was nervous. She feared seeing him and his turning away, refusing to talk to her like he'd done before. For the first time she consciously considered why he hadn't written to her for the many months she was in Stratford. Could he still be upset? But that was impossible, there was no reason for it.

On the first Sunday after her return Judith prepared for church, brushing her hair until it was shiny and smooth, going over in her head what she would say to Cuthbert the moment they were alone. She imagined herself with hands clasped together, begging forgiveness. All through the service she daydreamed about rekindling their walks together and sharing a few hours in each other's company. Shamefully, she imagined his kiss and the touch of his hand. After the service Judith looked for Cuthbert as the congregation filed out, but she never saw him. She lingered on the grounds for a couple of hours, not knowing what else to do with herself, but Cuthbert never showed up. Eventually, Judith walked back to the Mountjoys', defeat in every step.

Judith decided that she couldn't wait for another Sunday to pass to see Cuthbert. She had to find him sooner than that, even if it meant showing up at the Bull and talking to him in front of their friends. It'd been so long since she'd seen the Leicester's Men, James with the kind eyes that had witnessed so much, Tarlton with the mischievous grin and uncanny impressions, Wilson with the brooding temperament and few, but incisive observations, and of course Robert Greene, her ready confidant and friend. She looked forward to seeing them all, but at the same time, she wasn't prepared for questions about her return, and she certainly hadn't planned on her initial reunion with Cuthbert being in front of everyone. She considered all her options but in the end decided she didn't have any other choice. She simply couldn't wait any longer to find him.

When Judith walked into the Bull the following evening, her now unaccustomed eyes stung from the burnt, smoky air. She blinked and wiped her face, searching the overcrowded room, patrons bumping into her as she stood awkwardly near the front door. She spied the Leicester's Men at a table near the back of the hall and her heart skipped a beat when she saw that Cuthbert was indeed with them, hunched over, listening to Laneham relate an animated story. She walked towards her friends, noting that Cuthbert looked healthy and strong and fully recovered from his sickness. As she got closer, the nearness of him took her breath away.

"By my eyes, 'tis Judith!" Greene cried.

The rest of the troupe called out their welcome and the hearty greetings comforted her. Laneham and Perkin made room in the center of the bench and she sat down between them. Cuthbert looked elsewhere.

"We were sure you'd been married off by now," Clarke said. "Where've you been?"

"'Twas my brother that was betrothed, not me," Judith laughed. "I went home for the wedding, but I'm back now. Free and most certainly unbonded." She tried to catch Cuthbert's eye but he continued to look anywhere but at her. "Nay, not me."

"Methinks the lady doth protest too much," Clarke joked, a smile in his eyes. "I thought all women eagerly anticipated their wedding day."

"That proves how little you know about women."

The banter continued for some time, but Cuthbert never joined in and Judith couldn't help but grow increasingly anxious to hear even a small word from him. Having refused to look her way the entire evening Cuthbert finally stood up, smiled tightly, and mumbled, "good morrow" to the group before turning and heading for the door.

Judith must have looked panic stricken for Greene whispered, "Go. Go after him."

Judith caught up with Cuthbert on a thin, winding street a few blocks from the pub. It was cold outside and she had left her cloak behind, but she barely felt a thing.

"Cuthbert, wait!" The strength of her voice arrested his step, but still Cuthbert wouldn't turn around to face her. "It's been so long. And I've missed you so much." She struggled to regain her breath and Cuthbert took a step forward. "Wait! Cuthbert. Why are you leaving? What have I done?"

Slowly Cuthbert turned, raised his eyes and looked at Judith. For the first time her pretty face seemed to him ill-seeming, thick, bereft of beauty.

"Cuthbert."

"I won't be made a fool of. By you, or by any lowly woman."

Judith shook her head in wonderment.

"I know," Cuthbert said, "about you and Greene. I saw the two of you together." Like pain seeping out of a freshly opened wound his words at last flowed out. "How could you? Betray me with another man? With a *friend*, even? I cared for you, more than I have for any other woman, more than I even thought was possible. But not any longer. To think that you were keeping me at a distance with your pretty little laugh and your dainty little hands when at the very same time you weren't showing any hesitation whatsoever with Greene. D'you think I'm dumb, Judith, is that it? Did 'ye think I would grovel at your feet?"

Judith tried to understand what Cuthbert was saying. "But I've always been true to you Cuthbert. I don't understand. There's never been anyone else, it has always been you, only you."

Cuthbert guffawed in disbelief.

"Do you think I had an affair with Robert Greene? Is that what you're saying? But we can go back inside and ask him right now." Judith half-turned towards the pub but Cuthbert made no effort to join her. "Besides, Greene is your friend, he wouldn't do anything like that. Why would you even think such a thing?"

Cuthbert strode towards Judith. In a sudden, quick movement he grabbed her by the waist and kissed her. But this was not the reunion kiss Judith had been imagining. This was a hard, cruel, painful embrace.

"Stop it. Cuthbert, you're hurting me."

"So you'll give yourself to him, to that old man with the red beard that sleeps with every woman from here to Cambridge, but me, the man you claim to love, you'll not even lay with once?"

Tears streamed from Judith's eyes. "I have never slept with Robert Greene. I have never slept with any man," though here she seemed to pause. "I would never betray you Cuthbert, no matter what you think. I love you."

The note of defeat in Judith's voice seemed to confirm Cuthbert's assessment of the situation. He didn't want to hear any more. He was upset Judith had returned from Stratford at all, and reminded him of these humiliating emotions. Disgusted at the whole situation, Cuthbert turned and determinedly strode away.

That evening Judith's sleep was tormented with dreams of Cuthbert as a soldier in battle, fighting and eventually losing his life to a brutal Spanish soldier who gleefully stuck his sword into Cuthbert's breast over and over again. When Judith woke her heart was pounding and the sheets were clinging to her pasty skin.

In the early morning light, however, once she'd regained her senses and thought things through, she convinced herself that things weren't so bad. At least now she knew what had been bothering Cuthbert all this time. It should be easy, she thought as she got dressed and combed her hair, to fix things. Get everyone together - Cuthbert, Greene, and herself - and have Greene admit that nothing untoward was going on. Once Cuthbert understood that it was Mrs. Mountjoy who invited Greene to the house that day in the garden, he wouldn't be upset. Once he knew Greene had been there to help with her writing, maybe he would even read some of her plays himself. Judith was optimistic, imagining a future scenario where she, Cuthbert, Greene, and even the rest of the Leicester's Men, all sat around a table discussing how best to put her plays on the stage.

There was a knock on the door and Judith, assuming it was Joan returning with a fresh jug of water, wondered why she didn't just walk right in. Opening the door, a greeting ready on her lips, Judith was startled to see Mrs. Mountjoy standing in the hall.

"I received a letter this morning," she said matter-of-factly, "from your father."

Judith's hands prickled with sweat as she turned to let Mrs. Mountjoy into the room.

"He tells me you're betrothed to a local man and that you ran away from home."

"I am not bethrothed. I never agreed to marry that man."

Mrs. Mountjoy sighed. "Well, they are expecting you back in Stratford before the week is out. I can't keep you here, Judith, you know that. I would like to," she offered sympathetically, "but we Huguenots must avoid scandal at all costs. You need to at least go home and try to work this out." Mrs. Mountjoy looked thoughtfully out the window. "If you really don't want to get married, my dear, there are ways of making a man uninterested."

Judith tried to smile. "I know."

Mrs. Mountjoy turned from the window. "You can stay here for a little while longer, but then, you must return to your family."

Judith understood that she didn't have much time. She had to figure out a way to stay in London. A twinge of guilt over her family's debt tugged at her, but she let it slip away. She went over her options and realized that the only real possibility for staying in London was to ask James for a job. She'd been to the Theater so many times, she knew the stage and all their productions inside and out, that she could easily do the job of a stage hand. She could prepare props, set cues, and clean up after performances. She knew that a woman had never been hired before, never even been considered in fact for such a job, but she also knew that she could do it better than anyone James had ever hired before. And she felt positive that she could convince him of that. Eventually, maybe she could even interest him in her plays and he could have her write for the Theatre - though it made her nervous to think so big. The more she thought about working at the Theatre as a stage hand, however, the more excited she got. It was her destiny, she imagined, to be surrounded by actors and strive every day to make people laugh and feel entertained. Judith began to believe that her entire life up until that point, Master Hunt and everything, had all been necessary to lead her here; to lead her to London, to the Theater, and of course also to Cuthbert. It would all work out, she reassured herself, it had to.

Wasting no time Judith went that afternoon to a performance of *The Three Ladies of London*. As in days past, she waited until the entire audience had left and James had closed up the pit, and then she accompanied the Leicester's Men on their walk to the Bull. She didn't expect Cuthbert to show up that evening, but it didn't matter, as Judith's purpose wasn't to talk to him this time, but to his father.

She caught up with James as they walked down Bishopsgate.

"Judith," James said, glancing over his shoulder at her.

"I enjoyed tonight's performance," she said, clearing her throat. "The dialogue in the second act, of the general just before he beheads the prisoner-of-war, was moving."

"I'm glad to hear you liked it," James said, his eyebrow raised. "And?"

"And?"

"Usually you offer criticism, Judith, not praise. I'm waiting for the 'but'," he added, smiling.

Judith's cheeks bloomed red and she didn't know what to say.

"'Tis fine," James reassured her, "I don't always agree with what you have to say, but I like your opinions. Not everyone has the confidence to offer me the truth." They turned down Black Alley and Judith realized she only had a few more blocks before they'd be at the pub.

"I really had no complaints about this one."

James could tell that Judith was nervous so he changed the topic of conversation.

"How was your trip to Stratford? Was it good to see your family again?"

"Yay," Judith mumbled, "of course." She took a breath. "But Stratford is no longer my home, London is. I realized that on this journey. I could never live anywhere else but London - the busyness, the excitement, the Theatre," Judith swung her arms open to indicate everything around her.

James nodded, understanding her love of the city.

"I would do anything to stay here," she continued. "I would do anything to make the Theatre my home."

James stopped walking and looked at Judith quizzically.

"I know 'tis uncommon, Mr. Burbage, and maybe it'll strike you as odd, but I also know you appreciate the value of a good worker. I was wondering, do you think you could hire me as a stage hand? I'd do an excellent job - you know I know the Theatre and that stage better than anyone. I know how the light reflects in the different corners, where the hollow spots are that swallow the voices, which patrons must be turned away before they get through the doors, and what to say if the authorities come for a visit."

"Well then you know," James added, "that the authorities wouldn't like it if I hired a woman stage hand. Already we're in trouble for not being guilded. And lies are constantly spread that we're an indecent institution, encouraging crime, bad morals, and heretical thoughts. Can you imagine what they'd say if I hired a woman?"

"But I'm a hard worker," Judith argued. "I'd do a good job, better than any of your other stage hands."

"'Tis probably true," James admitted, while thinking to himself that that would only inspire jealousy and dissent among the current stage hands. "But would you truly be happy working at the Theatre with a bunch of men?"

"Yay, I would. I know I would."

James seemed skeptical. "I think not. You'd be bored as a stage hand, and what next? Do you wish to act on the stage as well?" James thought he was getting at the real nature of Judith's request.

"Nay, nay, I would never suggest that," Judith said, horrified. "Just work for you, behind the scenes, doing everything I can to make the Theatre a success."

James was silent.

"Mr. Burbage, please. You need not pay me much, just enough for room and board. I only wish to avoid having to return to Stratford."

James looked again at Judith and for the first time he no longer saw the sweet, innocent, eager young fan that flocked to all their performances. For the first time she looked rather wan and needy, like one of the hanger-ons who always wanted something of him, a job, some money, a little affection. It made him so tired.

James began walking again and when they arrived at the Bull he told Judith that he'd think about it and let her know. For the first time, however, he didn't hold the door open for her as she went to step inside the pub.

Within a day word had spread through the Leicester's Men that Judith had asked for a job, for actual money-paying employment with the Theatre. Her status among the troupe dropped precipitously; she was no longer the entertaining, pretty, welcome guest, whose presence at the Bull was treated with good humor and camaraderie, she was now a leech, a parasite, an imposter, a sponge, a Judas, an outsider, a woman. She continued to show up, unaware at first at the loss of good will she'd engendered, but it finally dawned on her when her contributions to the conversations were routinely denigrated, and when even kind Laneham stopped making room for her at the table.

Wilson was ecstatic; he couldn't have asked for a better turn of events. Cuthbert had clearly refused her, James had finally gotten annoyed with her, and even Greene, her best friend among the group, seemed not to know what to do with her any longer. Wilson had always known that Judith didn't fit in their world, that she belonged where all women belonged, at home and out of the way, and now things were finally ending up in their rightful place. He could tell that soon Judith would realize this too and return to Stafford, or whatever the hell stupid town it was she came from.

Judith remained dumbfounded. All of a sudden she seemed to have lost her friends and her place in the world felt uncertain. She couldn't quite figure out what had happened to make it so. The Theatre was successful, every year it made more and more money. James was always complaining about the stage hands and how he needed more help. She'd been sure her friends would be happy to have her around, a permanent member of the group. She went over things in her head but simply couldn't understand why everyone suddenly disliked her. Something was missing, something didn't make sense, and she had to figure it out soon if she was going to find a way to stay in London for much longer.

Desperate, Judith sought out Cuthbert. She yearned for his consolation, his friendship, his help. He would understand what was happening and he could tell her the truth; he'd always been so good at explaining the world to her and describing the underlying motivations of men. And Judith refused to believe that deep down, he didn't still care for her. Cuthbert was the key, she thought, and she had to speak with him.

The problem was that he no longer went to the Bull and she doubted he was going to show up at church again unless he was certain she wasn't there. He was avoiding her, and the only way to see him was to force a confrontation. That night, as Judith had done once before, she pretended to fall asleep next to Joan as the dark evening hours passed into night. Once the house was completely silent she slipped out of bed, stepped outside into the algid air, and made her way to the Burbage house. The front door was again unlocked and she made her way up the stairs and into Cuthbert's bedroom. This time, however, he woke the minute she stepped across the threshold.

"Who goes there?" Cuthbert called out, reaching for his sword.

"'Tis me, Judith. Shhhh," She rushed to Cuthbert's side and held his arm back. He yanked it away and sat up in bed.

"What in the lord's name?"

"Please. Not so loud."

Cuthbert stared at Judith in amazement.

"I have to speak with you," Judith said, trying not to shiver. It'd been bitterly cold outside and, yet again, she'd forgotten to wear her cloak. "I need your help. I need to stay in London."

Cuthbert was mute, staring at Judith's thin, vulnerable frame.

"I beg you, will you speak to your father for me?" Judith bowed her head and shifted on the floor by Cuthbert's bed. When he didn't say anything, she looked up. "I asked him to hire me on at the Theatre, as a stagehand, but he seems hesitant. I think," she said, trying to gauge Cuthbert's reaction, "it may be out of loyalty to you. And if you told him it'd be ok, he would hire me. I need a job, Cuthbert. I can't go back to Stratford. Please. Will you help me?"

Cuthbert repositioned himself, backing away further from Judith. "Why should I help you?" he finally asked.

"Because I have no one else to turn to," Judith said, beginning to cry. Suddenly everything seemed so overwhelming. "I don't know what to do anymore and I always used to know what to do. I used to know how to make people laugh and cry, I used to know what I was good at and what I wasn't, I used to know what people thought of me and if they liked me, but I realize now that I know nothing." She stopped to catch her breath. "I was once so certain that everything would work out, that life would work out, and now I have no idea what is happening."

The ice around Cuthbert's heart thawed slightly. For a moment he felt the desire to reach out and comfort Judith's small, blond head, but he waited until the feeling passed. He recalled the promises he'd made himself to never be fooled again, and he reeled in his slowly unwinding compassion. "I can't tell my father what to do."

Judith looked at him, the tears streaming from her eyes, "You could try."

Cuthbert shook his head and looked away.

"Forgive me," Judith pleaded, "I'm sorry for hurting you, for leaving London, for not proving to you how much I loved you. I am so sorry," she hiccuped. "But you can't stay angry at me forever. We love each other. How can you ignore what it feels like to be together? Are you really going to pretend that you feel nothing for me? Are you really going to throw everything away?"

"You're the one who threw it away."

"But Cuthbert I swear, you've been misled. I have never been unfaithful to you - ever."

Cuthbert recalled Wilson's words, that Judith would never admit to anything and that he should not believe anything she said. This was exactly the situation he'd been warned about. He looked at Judith, trying to decide how to respond, when he saw her shiver from the cold. Instinctively, he pulled back the covers.

Judith's tears dried up as she looked from the bed, to Cuthbert, and back to the bed again. She was quite cold, but she also knew that she shouldn't get into bed next to Cuthbert. Then she wondered if this was his offer of forgiveness; if he was giving her an opening, a chance to talk things over a little longer while warming her cold limbs.

Judith slipped under the covers. It was so warm and cozy beside Cuthbert's strong, familiar body that she couldn't help but press her legs up against him. She laid her head on his shoulder and closed her eyes, comforted at last.

Cuthbert was a swirl of emotions. He wanted to keep what was happening at a distance, but with Judith's soft body so close to his, it was impossible to stay in control. From the moment she'd walked into the room he'd been aroused, and now his desire only grew. All he could think about was grabbing Judith and touching her and loving her once again. He turned towards her and kissed the top of her head. The sweet smell of her hair made things worse and, unable to help himself, he slipped his hand around her belly and down across her thighs.

Judith stirred. "Wait. Cuthbert. No."

But he didn't hear her. Thunder raged in his ears as he kissed Judith's neck and climbed on top of her. He'd dreamt of this moment so many times he couldn't count. He'd imagined Judith's look of pleasure as he made love to her so often he was certain he saw it now. When he went for her lips, he was surprised when she turned her head to the side. He tried again and this time he heard her protest.

Cuthbert pulled back, anger flaring up in his chest. "What? Am I still not good enough?"

Judith struggled to put her passions in place and sit up in the bed. "Nay, it's just– we just–" she stumbled, her face hot, "shouldn't." Judith wanted to give in to Cuthbert, she yearned for the feel of his touch on her skin, but she'd been told so many times that this was wrong, and she was trying now to get her life in order, not make it more messy. She touched Cuthbert's arm but he pulled away, shifting himself so he sat off the side of the bed with only his profile remaining visible. He gripped the wood of the bed until his knuckles ached.

No one said a thing as the floorboards in the house creaked and a bird flew dangerously close to the window. Finally Cuthbert broke the silence. "Please leave." The tone of his voice had changed from anger to weariness. "I need you...to leave."

The note of resignation in Cuthbert's voice broke Judith's heart. She couldn't believe he'd give up on them so easily, that the strong, passionate, determined man she knew would reach a place with her and just retreat. She inched closer to him on the bed but he didn't seem to notice. She moved closer still and encircled his back with her body, resting her head on his strong, broad shoulder. "I love you," she whispered.

He turned to face her and she drank in his deep, dark eyes. For the first time in a long time Judith felt like she was where she was supposed to be; she felt safe, things felt right. She never wanted to lose this feeling of warmth, or take the chance of losing Cuthbert ever again. She leaned in towards him and kissed his lips. When Cuthbert grabbed her by the waist and brought her back onto the bed she opened her legs to him like she knew he'd always wanted.

15

The next day Judith sat in the servant's quarters darning socks and remembering the night with Cuthbert all over again, when a letter arrived from Stratford. It looked to be from her brother, William, and Judith's hands shook as she opened it. In truth, she was surprised he hadn't written earlier.

> *Judith,*
>
> *Your sleeping pallet lies empty and rumors fly that you've been carried off by wolves. Baby Edmund keeps asking when you're coming home, poor Joan doesn't know how to answer him, and even the animals seem subdued in their movements, knowing that something is amiss. Where are you?*
>
> *We of course got your note that you were "unable" to marry Richard, but the burning question is, why? Is it Richard? Are you afraid of marriage? Has something else happened entirely? The neighbors have all*

assumed the worst and mother is running around trying to convince them otherwise. I'm guessing you are fearful of the responsibility of married life, of having to obey a new master, of not having your future blank before you any longer to do with as you please, to dream with as you want. In truth, I understand this hesitation. That is why I finally decided to write you this letter. I never told anyone, but I didn't sleep at all the night before my wedding to Anne. I was tormented with the notion that there was no going back, that marriage puts you on a different path in life, a path from which there is no return and no looking back. And if you make a mistake, what can be done? Nothing. Absolutely nothing as marriage is a bond before God, inseverable, tied forever. It would make anyone nervous.

However, this is a path that we all must travel, even you my dear sister, at some point. It was not meant to be avoided, but braved, nay, even embraced. I have found a good and loving match in Anne and, I do believe that Richard would be a good match for you. He has a fiery spirit which rivals your own - something I sometimes think you need.

The good news is that mother has assiduously worked to reassure Richard that you will be back soon and that nothing improper has happened, and she has extracted from him a promise to still have you when you do. I feel it my duty to also remind you that father is hanging from a tether hook with the town council, due to all the raids from the religious police. Please don't heap further scandal upon our family by failing to return; your mysterious disappearance only gives our enemies more ammunition.

Finally, Anne insists that I add that she is looking forward to becoming as close to you as a blood sister. You have ready friends and family here that love you and miss you. Everything will be alright if you just

> *return home - do not let the demons of the unknown*
> *stand in the way of the path to your future; do not let*
> *fear usurp duty; come home.*

> *William*

Judith reread the letter twice and then crumpled it in her hand. It was the first time she'd ever thrown away a letter. Usually she treasured them, for the words they contained, for the emotions they revealed, from a sense of respect for the expensive ink and paper they were written on. But Judith was never going to want to read that letter again. She had no way of answering it. She knew she was disappointing her brother, her family, years of tradition, but she also knew that she simply couldn't return to Stratford. She was drawn to London, to the Theatre, to Cuthbert, like a tiller to a rutted course in the soil. There was no way off the track, there was no way she could turn around and go back or head up some different path; her course was set.

Judith got up from where she sat and threw the letter in the open hearth. It burned surprisingly quickly. When there was nothing left of even the red wax seal Judith returned to her seat, picked up her work, and continued darning. She didn't prick herself once as she finished the pile of socks, though tears clouded her vision.

That night Judith couldn't sleep. In the bed next to Joan she tossed and turned, trying to quiet the demons in her mind. Joan didn't appear to be having an easy night either, kicking the sheets and calling out for cheese and strawberry jam. A little past midnight Judith got out of bed, stood by the window, and contemplated the streets of London, looking for some sort of sign to tell her what to do. All she saw were the dark, scurrying rats of London, come to dine on the sewage and waste of the city she loved so much. She stood by the window till her fingers were numb with cold and then, finally, turned and slipped back under the covers.

Judith came to the conclusion that if she could just prove herself, that if she could just write and perform one great play in her lifetime, all would be forgiven. Her family would come to see her talent and her destiny and know, later if not now, that not marrying Richard had been the right decision and that London was the place for her. She ached with the desire not to disappoint anyone, and she hated thinking about the pain she was causing her father and mother and the rest of her family, but she couldn't walk away from the only thing she knew how to do. It would be like asking her mother to walk away from her faith, or the Queen to walk away from her country - impossible.

The next day Judith was summoned by the master of the house. Mr. Mountjoy travelled so often it was rare for him to spend time with the servants or worry himself about the internal workings of the house, so when he asked Judith to come see him in his office, she knew it was serious. Her stomach knotted with fear as Mr. Mountjoy frowned and asked her how much longer she intended to stay with them.

"Not long, sir," she curtsied deeply. "Just until I get a job."

"You intend to work for another family?" Mr. Mountjoy asked, perplexed. He'd been told that Judith was to return to her family in Stratford to get married; that she was having some sort of feminine hesitation about it, but that she just needed to be prodded a little into leaving and returning home. He could relate to her fears, he'd been hesitant before his own marriage and look how it had turned out.

"Nay, forgive me. I meant, just a few more days. I promise, I'll not stay much longer."

"You know I like you Judith," Mr. Mountjoy said kindly. "You work hard, you're a sweet girl, and Mrs. Mountjoy seems entertained by you well enough, which is always rather important," his voice trailed off. "I would like to keep you, I would, I just can't. You know that, right? No servant, not even one as pretty as you, is worth a potential inquiry by the town council."

"I know," Judith said, nodding her head. "I am sorry to be so much trouble."

Mr. Mountjoy appreciated the apology, while waving it away.

"Thank you for your kindness," Judith added.

Mr. Mountjoy smiled. He opened the door for Judith to leave the room, but before letting her out he added impulsively, "You can take a little time to get your things in order. But then you need to return to your family and to your betrothed. You will make a fine wife, Judith, worry not."

Judith left the room, shivering with cold. She knew her days in the Mountjoy house were numbered, she'd always known that she couldn't stay there forever, but Mr. Mountjoy's kind demeanor, his obvious discomfort at having to get involved in such an affair, drew Judith to him. He was a kind man and this was a kind house. She hated having to leave it. At the same time, her heart lifted at the realization that she'd just been given not a few more days, but a few more weeks reprieve.

Judith used the time well. She worked assiduously editing, writing, and reworking her best play, the one she tentatively called "Romeo and Juliet." She still believed she could convince James and the rest of the Leicester's Men of the talent of her work, if she could just find enough time to polish it. After a few weeks of constant effort, skipping meals and ignoring Joan every time she peered over her shoulder and tried to grab a page of her work, Judith felt that the writing had advanced to a stage where she could ask Greene to come to the house, read the latest draft, and giver her his honest opinion.

When Greene showed up, chilled by the winter air which seemed harsher and bitterer than any in recent memory, he walked straight to the hearth and warmed his hands by the fire. As soon as he was comfortable Greene turned to Judith and began the conversation by asking after Mrs. Mountjoy.

"The mistress is well, thank you," Judith told him.

"Is she here today?"

"Nay, not today."

"On a cold day such as this? I was sure she'd stay home by the fire."

"Yes, well, Mrs. Mountjoy is not one to let the cold stop her social engagements. I believe she's lunching with Lady Spencer."

Greene nodded, but looked about him distracted.

Judith fumbled with her papers, thrusting them in Greene's direction. "Will you take a look at it? Will you read my latest play and let me know, honestly, what you think?"

Greene sat in a chair and put on his spectacles. He read for less than a minute, then glanced over his eye piece at Judith's anxious figure.

"Can I give you some advice?" he asked.

"Of course. 'Tis why I asked you here."

"Go home."

Judith's heart sank like a brazier's weight.

"You're a good and earnest girl, Judith, no one can doubt that. And you may even have a little talent," he said, shaking the papers in his hand, "but your place isn't here. It's not in London and it certainly isn't with the Leicester's *Men*."

Judith blinked, but didn't say a word or move an inch from the edge of her seat.

"I admire your youth, Judith, I do. Your youth and vitality and earnestness, and even your naivete. But you have to understand that there are worlds of men, and there are worlds of women, and they àre separate worlds. Mixing them has never brought any benefit, nor made any man happy." Greene shifted in his seat, trying to find the best way to explain the truth as he saw it.

"Joan of Arc died at the stake. Cleopatra died on the throne, aye? Bitten by a poisonous snake."

Judith nodded dutifully.

"Their odysseys did not end well. God does not help women succeed who try to go beyond their place. It messes with the natural order of things. I tell you this not to dishearten you or make you sad," Greene said, reaching out and patting Judith's knee, "but to save you from greater heartache later. Go home and marry and have many happy children. Your disappointment in this will pass, and you will be more content in the long run, I promise you."

Judith tried to digest what Greene was telling her, but she was having a hard time taking it in. All she wanted was to write. She'd invited him here to read her plays, but somehow they'd gotten off track, like in one of their many pub conversations. How could she bring him around to focus on her work again? She knew that she was different, that not many women did things like write plays - but what did it matter? If her work was good, wasn't that the most important thing? If she could move audiences, wasn't that all that mattered?

"But how is the play?" Judith asked, pointing to the papers still in Greene's hands.

He looked down at them for a moment. "Judith," he said, looking up, "I don't have a good feeling about this. You're banging your pretty little head against a very thick wall. This will not end well for you," he added, somewhat off to the side. "Let it go."

Judith knew that Greene had always been her most ardent supporter. At the pub, with the other men, he'd always understood her point of view and listened to what she was trying to say in a way that no one else ever had, even Cuthbert. If Greene no longer supported her, she knew that she was lost. It was just that she was having a hard time understanding why. Why no one, even Greene now, would give her work a chance on its independent merits.

"I'm telling you this as a friend," Greene added softly.

Maybe Greene wasn't the right person to approach, Judith thought, maybe she should take her chances and go straight to James. He'd always appreciated her boldness of action and forthright opinions. Judith considered her next move as she nodded blankly in unison with Greene. She hoped she didn't seem too distracted or disappointed. She wished he would leave, if he was not going to read her play, because she only had so much time and she had to figure out how she was going to approach James and get him, at least, to take a real and honest look at her work.

Early the next morning Judith woke with a headache and a feeling of nausea rising from the pit of her stomach. She sat up in bed and swallowed hard, putting the back of her hand to her forehead, then sliding her palms beneath her armpits to check for lumps. It was habit, whenever the slightest illness came on, to check for lumps beneath your arms and in your groin; you never could be too careful over the possibility of the plague. But there were no portending growths and after a minute the nausea passed too. With a feeling of relief Judith got out of bed and dressed for the day. She didn't think about counting until she was halfway down the stairs on her way to the kitchen.

Ever since her encounter with Master Hunt many years ago Judith had been a regular counter. Her mother had explained to her the appropriate length of time between bleeds and had told her what to look for in those first few weeks after being with a man; what the signs were that confirmed whether you were with child. Even though Judith had never been with anyone since Master Hunt, she had always taken comfort in counting the days and welcoming her bleeds, knowing for certain that another month had passed and she was not yet burdened with a bairn. Standing there on the stairs she counted again now, and realized that the numbers weren't right. For the first time, her bleeds were late.

Sweat broke out on Judith's forehead as she thought about the enormity of what this meant. Desperately Judith tried to convince herself that perhaps she was just starting a winter cold, a passing flu that would move on in a few days. But the more Judith listened to the internal workings of her body, the more she knew the truth. Her lower back hurt and her breasts ached, her nipples were oddly sensitive. All the signs pointed to what she didn't want to admit - that she was pregnant.

Judith turned and went back up the stairs and quietly reentered the bedroom, not wanting to disturb Joan. She leaned against the wall, and then slid down to the floor, her head between her knees. She sat for many minutes thinking.

She tried to imagine Cuthbert's reaction if she told him - a smile? a frown? blanket confusion? - but it was impossible. One minute she was able to picture him graciously offering his hand in marriage, the next it was his back, turned on her once again in anger. They were in such a perilous state right now, she didn't know what to think and she dreaded adding this to the brew. She knew what her mother would say, her mother would tell her to return to Stratford and marry Richard, quick, before the pregnancy was discovered. But Judith couldn't imagine lying to a child, for years, about who its actual father was. She knew she could never live with the deception. And then fear struck her heart because, deep down, she also knew that Cuthbert really might not take her in, and if he didn't, she had absolutely nowhere to go.

"I have to speak with you," Judith whispered to Cuthbert as she approached him on the doorstep of his house. She'd been waiting all morning to catch him as he stepped outside. Cuthbert looked around, startled, and then considered Judith's figure standing before him. It was a bright, cold January day and his cheeks stung with the chill.

"'Tis not the best day for a walk," Cuthbert said, rubbing his hands together. Much of the snow had melted from the city streets and rooftops, but the ground was still rock hard and the wind wasn't much for lingering.

"We could go to the Garter, have some tea."

Cuthbert grimaced. The Garter was where gamblers and drunks met, it was a dirty place, a dark place, a place where you went to find a whore. Cuthbert wondered why Judith would even be familiar with the place.

"We'll be undisturbed there," she said, reading his mind. "We won't see anyone we know."

Cuthbert doubted that, but he was willing to go along. He turned and walked with Judith as they made their way to the pub.

Inside the Garter it was dark and comfortably warm, but crowded. Judith was surprised to see so many people, having imagined the place more desolate than this. Cuthbert directed her to a table near the back and they sat down together.

"You haven't come to the Bull much lately," Judith said, not knowing where to begin, "though I haven't been there myself much either these past few weeks."

Cuthbert shrugged in response.

"I've missed you," Judith offered, putting her hand on the table. She hoped Cuthbert would reach across the divide and take her hand in his, but he didn't. He seemed distracted.

"Did you want to talk about something? Because I really should be going if not."

Judith ignored the brusque tone. What they had to talk about was important and it was just that Cuthbert didn't know it yet. Gathering her courage she leaned forward, took a breath, and told him of her condition.

Cuthbert leaned away and into his chair. His expression, one she hadn't imagined, was ironical. "How now?" he said, as if

185

seeking clarification. Cuthbert couldn't believe Judith was pulling this on him. He'd heard of women who seduced you and then demanded money, marriage, or some other form of blackmail to "avoid" a pregnancy, but Cuthbert had never imagined Judith the type.

Judith repeated herself, a little louder this time. Cuthbert dropped forward on the legs of his chair.

"Are you certain?"

She nodded.

Cuthbert looked at the delicate face and smooth hair that he'd once loved so much and wondered why god saw fit to put such an evil force in so pretty a package. For Cuthbert didn't believe Judith for a moment. After she had come to his house in the middle of the night, and slept with him like any common whore, she'd lost all credibility in his eyes. It'd been a little surprising, in fact, how quickly his obsession with her had ended once he had had her. And now he no longer felt guilty about it, because this made it clear that Judith had only come to him as part of a plan to force him into marriage.

"And you think it's mine?"

Judith didn't understand the question at first. When Cuthbert repeated it, her face grew hot. She realized in that instant how little they actually trusted each other - if he could ask her such a question, he had never really known her, and if she was surprised by such a question, then she had greatly overestimated him. The weight of what was happening pressed down on Judith like a wet cloak and tears sprung to her eyes, she couldn't help it.

Cuthbert relented a little. "Maybe 'tis too soon to tell," he offered. "When were we together? One, two..., why it's only been three weeks, not even a month, you probably have it all wrong." Cuthbert knew nothing about the ways of women, except that he'd overheard his mother once talking about her *monthly* cycle.

But Judith knew. She knew that she was pregnant and she knew that she had lost Cuthbert. Something she had done, somewhere, at some time, had made him turn from her. She would probably never know what it was that she had done wrong, but looking into his familiar brown eyes, distracted and constantly darting to the side, she knew with certainty that he had turned from her, if she had ever really had him in the first place. She felt a gaping hole yawn beneath her.

"I can give you some money," Cuthbert said, discomfited by Judith's tears and lack of argument. He searched around and found a few coins in his purse and pressed them into her palm. Still, Judith didn't say anything, and Cuthbert grew annoyed she didn't appreciate the offering. "I can find you some more, if it's money you want."

Judith closed her hand around the few coins and shook her head. She couldn't look at Cuthbert any longer, it was too painful. After another moment of silence he stood up. "I'll be going then," he said abruptly, adding some excuse. His loud, departing footsteps rang like a toll in Judith's ears.

By the time she returned home, after having walked the streets of London for many cold hours, Judith was chilled as an icicle and her mind was frozen in a haze of disappointment and confusion. The worst had happened, Cuthbert had rejected her, and now she had no idea what she was going to do. She stood at the door of the Mountjoy house, numb with uncertainty, unable to lift her hand to the handle. She could still ask James to read her work, she could turn around right now and try to find him at the Bull, but it was a Sunday and he wouldn't be there, he would be at home, with his family, sitting down to a warm meal and wide smiles from his children. Besides, he would reject her too, she finally understood that. Judith leaned forward and pressed her forehead against the hard wood of the door. The cold seeped into her skin and down the back of her neck. If she couldn't stay in London with a proper job, what else was there? To be honest, even if she could stay in London, now that she was with child, what else was there? Her ears tingled and the tip of her nose crinkled with frost. She couldn't very well live here on her own and have a child on her own. Her mind had difficulty even imagining the possibility.

Judith stepped into the house and quietly made her way to the bedroom she shared with Joan. She managed not to run into anyone in the hall or on the stairs, and for this Judith was grateful. Inside the room she took off her gloves and cloak and sat on the edge of the bed, looking out the window at the dank gray day. She remembered the day after Anne's funeral, when all the neighbors had left, when all the food had been eaten, and everyone was supposed to just go back to their previous lives. She had sat on the edge of Anne's bed, her hand on Anne's small soft pillow, and felt as though a blackness had covered the world. A treasure had been lost, a perfect, honest, heart-felt person with a heart of sunshine had disappeared, and nothing had ever been the same again.

Judith got up from the bed and went and picked up her quill and ink, resting unobtrusively in a corner of the windowsill. The bottle of ink was near frozen and she rubbed it for a minute in her thin, brusque hands. Then she brought out some paper and sat down at the desk. The difference between now, and when Anne died, was that now she had her writing. Now she could let it all out into a poem or a play. Judith looked out the window and watched as the day slowly turned to dusk. She lit a candle and shifted in her chair. She rearranged the paper and ink on the desk. She tested the quill, drawing a perfect circle in a corner of a piece of paper. After a few minutes, she added a second circle around the first one. Judith sat at the little wooden desk for hours trying to write something. But nothing came out.

Judith had had difficulty putting her thoughts onto paper in the past, but it had never been as acute as this. This blockage was painful. Judith stood up from the desk, rung her hands out, and then sat back down again. She drew triangles, squares, and little faces on the edge of the paper. When she couldn't stand it any longer she stood up, paced the room, fluffed out her pillow, rearranged her shoes. A couple of hours later Joan came into the room to get ready for bed, and when Judith saw her friend's tired face she decided to give up for the moment and rest. She slipped under the familiar covers and closed her eyes along with her roommate.

But she couldn't sleep. She lay on the uncomfortable pallet twisting and turning, tormented with thoughts of home, listening to Joan snore loudly beside her until she just couldn't stand it any longer. Judith got out of bed, returned to the desk, relit the candle, and sat there, trying to force the ideas to come. She gripped the quill and concentrated hard, expectant, ready, hopeful, the late evening hours passing, the quill never moving in her hand. When

Judith finally gave up for good she was exhausted. And defeated. If she couldn't even write, what else was there?

The next morning Judith's gaunt, pale face shocked Mrs. Mountjoy. "Herbs," she commanded, "we must send you to the apothecary to get some herbs." Judith was not to do anything that day, but rest and take medicinal potions and recover her health. It was time to stop all this nonsense about working in the Theater, bolster Judith up with food and rest, and send her back to Stratford where she could start life anew. No more of this drama, no more crazy plans for staying in London. For Judith's own good, Mrs. Mountjoy announced confidently, it was time to settle down and make a home back in her village. Mrs. Mountjoy was at last certain that this was the right path to take, but her new confidence and determination didn't infect Judith; instead, it only depressed her further. It seemed to Judith that all her friends were turning away from her, one after the other. The world was falling off in pieces, hour by hour, friend by friend.

Judith let Mrs. Mountjoy's wrap her in a heavy woolen shawl and place atop her head a plaited straw hat lined with fur. She listened, somewhat distractedly, as Mrs. Mountjoy reminded her to tell the apothecary about every single symptom she was having, even the ones that only just started. And then the door closed behind Judith and she had nothing to do but walk away from the house that for the past four years she had called home.

The frozen cobblestones pressed through the thin soles of Judith's shoes and she noted absently that she'd forgotten to change out of her house slippers. Her pace didn't quicken or slow, however, she just walked on with a measured stride despite the cold in her feet and the ache in her bones.

In a few minutes the apothecary's storefront came into view. But Judith didn't stop, she only paused momentarily to look in the window at the rows of glass bottles and darkly colored potions that had often drawn her curiosity in the past. She continued walking, straight ahead, past bakeries and bookshops, green grocers and milliners, through the winding streets that she'd grown to love so much, further south towards the edge of the city. For the first time, Judith didn't notice the children playing in the streets, nor did she turn her head when a homeless man asked her for money.

Eventually Judith found herself facing the London Bridge, the pathway out of the city and the gateway to a greater unknown. It was decorated brightly that day with the banners and flags of the Queen, but for once Judith didn't pay attention to the colorful decorations that fluttered in the wind. She hunched her shoulders into her shawl and proceeded across the bridge, the cold gusts of wind biting into her flesh and whipping her hair loose from underneath the hat about her head.

When she came to the end of the bridge she turned right, as if with a purpose, and continued walking until she came to a clearing on the south bank of the river where nothing had been built up and no people seemed to be about. She stood still for a minute gazing at the river Thames rushing, in all its mighty glory, on to other things.

The water moved with a purpose and a life all its own, as if it was quite busy to get on with things, and Judith felt jealous of its strength and apparent purpose. She imagined all the cities and towns the river passed through, all the lands it irrigated, all the people it cleansed, all the fish it gave home to. She thought she saw a family of trout, huddled together in a curve of the river, content, exactly where they were supposed to be. She watched as the river swept leaves, tree branches, and clumps of dirt effortlessly along on the journey. And she wished that she could be a part of the journey, a passenger in this life-force that was so obviously essential to the earth. Tears filled Judith's eyes as she thought about joining the river, and floating effortlessly on to another place.

From a distance James Burbage could see a figure standing by the riverbank, and he was surprised. There was never anyone else out this way, this far from the city, as there was no reason for it. The only purpose for his regular trips out here was to scout for cheap land for a new location for the Theatre. He didn't really have the money right now to build a new Theatre all his own, but he would someday. Despite the regularly voiced doubts of his wife he knew the time would come when he would have the independence to build his own building and own his own playhouse and when that day came, he wanted to have a place chosen for it. He'd been coming out to this stretch of land for the past few months, whenever he had a free afternoon or morning, and he was pretty certain that this was where his dream would be built, if land prices stayed low enough. The location was a little far from the city center, and on a cold or wet day some patrons might not want to walk that far out just to see a play, but by the time James could set up his own company he felt certain he'd be so popular that no one would be deterred by the distance. And in the summer, of course, it was a beautiful walk.

As James got closer to the solitary figure he realized, with a shock, that it was Judith. Immediately suspicious he wondered if she'd followed him out there to talk to him once again about working with the company. Annoyance flickered in his breast and he almost turned away, until he noticed how perilously close to the edge of the river she was standing, looking into it at her own reflection. And then, curiously, he watched as Judith turned and began walking up and down the river's edge, bending low and standing up again, then bending low and standing up. She was like a bird pecking for seeds. James advanced a few paces towards her until he understood that Judith was sizing and measuring up stones, and stuffing them into a pouch she'd made out of her folded-up apron. If this wasn't further proof that Judith was crazy, James thought, he didn't know what was. He thanked God he was not a woman, to be touched with so many of the giddy offences God had taxed their whole sex withal. He couldn't wait to tell everyone at the pub what he'd seen her doing now.

Judith's apron grew heavy as she piled it with as many rocks as she could find. At first she'd only chosen the larger rocks, things that would really weigh her down, but there weren't enough of those and after awhile she just began picking up anything, small pebbles, handfuls of dirt. The tears clouding her eyes made it difficult to see exactly what she was doing anyway, so she stopped being particular. When her apron was so distended it threatened to break loose from her waist Judith finally stopped, tied it more securely about her, and stood tall before the river. She glanced up the length and breadth of it and said a small prayer. She gazed one last time at the fair city in the distance, and then she thought about her mother and father and silently asked their forgiveness. She whispered a plea to God, all merciful, to look after her brothers and sisters. And then, before she could begin to second guess herself, she jumped into the swift rushing river.

When Judith's figure disappeared, James rushed forward to the river's edge. He wondered whether he had seen her jump, or if she had just fallen in. He wanted to believe that she had just slipped and fallen into the icy river, but in the depths of his soul he knew he had witnessed a suicide. Desperately he searched the waters for Judith's body, but he couldn't see it anywhere. The water was rushing past too fast, and the river's bottom was dark and murky. James thought, only briefly, about jumping in after her.

At first, the pain was unbearable. Judith could not believe that anything could be this cold; the water was like shards of glass slicing deep into her skin. Her numbness had passed and she could feel again, she realized, but this was almost too painful. And then, as the apron filled with rocks weighed her down, her skin deadened and her heart slowed its beating and peace washed over Judith with the waters. Her final thought was for her baby, sorry suddenly that it had to die too. If only her baby could have lived without its mother, she thought. And then, the world went black.

Did you find all the quotes?

The author of this text made sure to embed at least one Shakespeare quote (if not more) within the narrative of every chapter. Can you find them all?

Readers who email the complete list of quotes (including the names of the plays, sonnets, and poems from which they come) to lea@learachel.com will be eligible for entry into an annual Amazon.com gift card giveaway. (One entry per person.)

Readers that can identify all the Virgina Woolf references in the text are eligible for an additional free entry.

Lea Rachel is originally from Detroit, Michigan. Over the years she has attended writing workshops at the University of Michigan, Ann Arbor, the University of California, Los Angeles, and the University of Iowa. Currently she is a professor at the University of Missouri, St. Louis and lives in University City, Missouri with her husband and son.

You can find out more about Lea, including other writing projects, at www.learachel.com.

www.ingramcontent.com/pod-product-compliance
Lightning Source LLC
Chambersburg PA
CBHW020403030726
47496CB00007B/2273